GRAVE
MISTAKES

GRAVE MISTAKES

BY CARLY ANNE WEST
ART BY TIM HEITZ AND
ARTFUL DOODLERS

Scholastic Inc.

The publisher does not have any control over and does not assume any responsibility for author or third-party websites or their content.

No part of this publication may be reproduced, stored in a retrieval system, or transmitted in any form or by any means, electronic, mechanical, photocopying, recording, or otherwise, without written permission of the publisher. For information regarding permission, write to Scholastic Inc., Attention: Permissions Department, 557 Broadway, New York, NY 10012.

This book is a work of fiction. Names, characters, places, and incidents are either the product of the author's imagination or are used fictitiously, and any resemblance to actual persons, living or dead, business establishments, events, or locales is entirely coincidental.

Library of Congress Cataloging-in-Publication Data available
ISBN 978-1-338-59429-4

10 9 8 7 6 5 4 3 2 1   20 21 22 23 24
Printed in the USA   23

First printing 2020
Book design by Cheung Tai

PROLOGUE

November 1965

Norman Darby chewed his bottom lip as his fingers pounded the keys, letters hammering their way onto the page. The ink was barely dry when he heard a growl from Mr. Cleave's office.

"Darby! If you moved any slower, you'd be traveling back in time! I need that feature *now*!"

"Al-almost done, Mr. Cleave," Norman called, his shoulders bunching their way to his ears. "Just putting the finishing t-touch—"

"It's the news, not Shakespeare, Darby. Give me the story!"

The *Raven Brooks Banner* was no place for the faint of heart. Norman had heard rumor of this, of course, but he could hardly have predicted the number of antacids he would take to beat back the daily heartburn his boss brought forth.

With an antacid on his mind, Norman squared his shoulders and stood up straight. *Today's the day, Norman,* he thought, working up the courage as he unfurled the last page of his article. *You're going to show him exactly who Norman Darby is—an investigative journalist.*

Norman made his way to Mr. Cleave's office. Mr. Cleave, however, did not even bother to look up.

Mr. Cleave's office was the stuff of nightmares, at least for Norman Darby. Norman woke up in a cold sweat at least twice a week as he dreamt of those beige filing cabinets, the thick wooden desk, the plastic plant that Norman could swear looked like it was on the verge of dying, even though it couldn't actually die. Maybe it just *wanted* to die. He dreamt about the brass paperweight Mr. Cleave never let out of his sight, not even for a second, not even to leave his office for a glass of water. But most of all, Norman's nights were haunted by the specter of Mr. Cleave, with his burly knuckles and a flattop so sharp, the edges of his hair could cut glass. And when Norman wasn't dreaming, well, he was at the office, seeing this all in person. Just like now.

Mr. Cleave lorded over his domain like a king, and Norman Darby was his ever-suffering servant.

But not today.

"Took long enough," Mr. Cleave growled, extending his hand for the copy, his eyes locked on the proof spread before him.

Norman took a slow, deep breath and handed the papers to his boss. He knew that this article could seal his fate forever—either as the hard-nosed investigative journalist he knew he was, or as the *Raven Brooks Banner*'s resident buffoon.

Mr. Cleave snatched the papers from Norman fast enough to slice a papercut through his finger, but Norman did not flinch. He didn't dare. Instead, he waited for his boss's reaction to the headline to which he'd given such careful consideration:

Norman didn't mean to hold his breath. He didn't even realize he was doing it until he started to wheeze. He hoped his inhaler was close by. He hoped Mr. Cleave would read the headline. Or maybe he didn't hope he would read the headline. The room was beginning to go bleary. Was it his imagination, or was that brass paperweight starting to glow?

Norman braced himself against the doorframe and had nearly decided to turn and walk away when the strangest thing happened.

Mr. Cleave looked up.

Norman Darby prided himself on his ability to read faces. He was a master at it. He could tell when a person was happy, when they were afraid, when they were lying through their teeth. It's part of what made him such a good investigative journalist.

But Mr. Cleave was the only person he had never been able to understand. His expressions never matched his tone. His responses didn't align to his motions. His eyes rarely matched the movements of his mouth.

He was, in a word, inscrutable.

And in this moment, Norman Darby had never found Mr. Cleave less readable.

They shared a strange silence in that moment. Maybe it was because he had been holding his breath for so long, but suddenly Norman felt sick.

Then, in the strangest exchange he had ever shared with

his boss, Mr. Cleave gestured to the chair on the other side of his imposing wooden desk.

"Mr. Darby, why don't you have a seat."

And then Mr. Cleave did something that Norman had never seen before, not even when the *Raven Brooks Banner* received its third award of the year or when one of the designers baked them all cheesecake brownies.

Mr. Cleave *smiled.*

Norman Darby began to lower himself into the chair across from his boss. This was it. This was the moment. *His* moment. Norman's boss—the inimitable Mr. Cleave—wanted to hear his ideas.

But before he could land in the chair, Mr. Cleave stopped him.

"Oh, and close the door, would you?"

Norman paused mid-squat, searching his boss's face for any sign he might have been wrong. Instead, he thought again he saw a glimmer of light emanate from the brass paperweight Mr. Cleave kept so closely guarded. But that was impossible, right?

Norman stood and closed the door.

Chapter 1

*L*ights behind my eyes.
   My head. My head.
   . . .

I'm gonna puke.

"Whoa! It's okay, Aaron, it's okay. We'll clean you up, just lie back down."

A guy in a pair of green scrubs is looking at the floor like he doesn't know what to do. His hands are outstretched at his side.

"Dr. Malcolm, is everything—oh . . ."

A woman in blue scrubs walks in and gets quiet. Her quietness permeates the room as if begging to be acknowledged.

"I barfed on him," I say and hang on to the edge of the bed, squeezing the thin mattress and fighting back another wave of nausea.

"I'll call maintenance," the nurse says and exits the room.

"A new set of scrubs, too," Dr. Malcolm calls after her.

Another set of feet squeak down the hall, and that sound, too, is unbearably loud. I squeeze my eyes shut and fall back onto the papery pillow behind me.

"Did he wake up? I thought I heard his—"

I recognize Dad's voice immediately, and I have no idea why, but the second he walks into the room, I start to cry. I'm suddenly four years old and terrified and confused, and only my dad can save me. I barely open my eyes. I shake with little silent sobs, and my head is killing me, but his arms are around my neck and he's pressing my head against him and he's shushing me like he used to when I'd have a nightmare.

This isn't a nightmare, though. I don't know what it is, but there's no question I'm awake.

I hear a set of wheels roll into the room, then the slap of a mop as it does its job, then the nurse as she hands the doctor a new set of clothes, then the doctor excusing himself while the nurse gently takes my arm, takes my blood pressure, takes my temperature, takes some blood with a needle, and takes her leave.

The entire time, my dad doesn't say a word; he simply shushes me, even after I've stopped crying. He keeps my head against him, cradled by his meaty forearm. He keeps his hand cupping my skull gently.

"Ah yes, all right, then," says the doctor when he comes back. Only then does my dad release me, and I let myself fall back to the pillow.

"Head injuries are rough," the doctor says, shaking his head slowly. "Hi, Aaron. I'm Dr. Malcolm."

Malcolm like my second-grade teacher. I think I can remember that.

Raven Brooks Hospital

Dr. Mathieu Malcolm

I feel my dad tense next to me. "Is he going to—?"

The doctor holds up his hands and tamps them down, pressing the worry away. "We've run all the tests, and so far, everything checks out. Aaron's going to make a full recovery. He just had a nasty fall."

A nasty fall.

If my brain didn't feel like it was clanging around in my head like a gong, maybe I'd be able to remember falling. From what? To where? My memory is a black hole.

Dad, on the other hand, appears to be up to speed, asking questions before I can form a complete thought.

"When can we take him home?" he asks.

"Assuming all checks out, tomorrow should be fine," Dr. Malcolm says.

It isn't long before the doctor and my dad are asking and answering questions, speaking in low voices that still hurt my head. All I can do is concentrate on the steady drip of the faucet coming from the sink in the bathroom by my bed. Its rhythmic drop into the drain echoes against my eyelids, and I try to use it as a way to meditate the pain away, but something about the patter of that drip is too familiar—too unnerving—to calm me.

Like it's echoing through a long, dank chamber.

Through a tunnel.

It all comes back in a wave—the tunnel leading from the weather station, the broken lantern that should have been in my grandparents' old office, the bloody smear across the wallet holding Mr. Gershowitz's ID.

Panic seizes me before I can catch it, and for just a moment I can't feel the blinding pain behind my eyes. I launch to a sitting position on the bed, grasping hold of my dad's arm and startling him out of his conversation with the doctor.

"Did you find it? The lantern in the tunnel? I fell through the wall, but I didn't mean to, and all of a sudden, I was running, or I think I was, it was just so dark, and I think there was someone else in there with me and . . . Dad, did you find his wallet? Mr. Gershowitz's wallet?"

"Aaron, calm down," Dad says quietly, prying my hand from his arm, but I can't stop myself. The questions are spilling out of me, and I urgently need them all answered.

"But did you find it?"

"Aaron," Dad hisses, his eyes widening as he discreetly turns his back to the doctor, covering me with his shadow. "I think you must be *imagining things.*"

His eyes are wide and his teeth are clamped shut, and I know that for some reason he wants me to shut up and nod my head, but I just *can't.*

"Hang on, did you say Gershowitz? As in *Ike* Gershowitz, that missing security guard?" Dr. Malcolm says from behind my dad.

Now both of them are casting their long shadows over my bed.

"Aaron, I think maybe you're just confused," Dad says, leaning a little closer to me. Any second now, I'm going to be vaporized. He faces Dr. Malcolm. "The fall from that tree was quite high."

I nod back.

"Yeah," I say. Dad's laser eyes lose some of their burn.

He turns to Dr. Malcolm. "My son's little friend—well, his father—works for the *Banner.* Every gruesome headline gets talked about. You know the stuff: robberies, disappearances, there's no censorship there . . . I'm sure Mr. Gershowitz's headline is the last thing he remembers," Dad says, shaking his head.

Dr. Malcolm seems only partly convinced. The crease between his brows deepens as he looks from my dad to me and back to my dad.

"Is it normal for him to be inventing memories like

this?" Dad asks, and just like that, he almost has me thinking he's genuinely concerned about my sanity.

Dr. Malcolm considers this. "Well, it's not unheard of. The brain is mysterious. So much we still don't know about it. Head injuries are different for everyone."

"Then he's going to be okay?"

Dr. Malcolm's face softens at Dad's concern. "Mr. Peterson, your son will be just fine. He needs some rest and more monitoring. I'll give you two a little space, but then it's time to say good night."

Dad nods cooperatively and shakes Dr. Malcolm's hand. The doctor gives my foot a gentle pat over the covers before leaving us alone.

Dad turns so fast, it's like he's on a hinge.

"Now, what's this about *tunnels*?"

There are very few things I know for certain right now. I know that my name is Aaron Peterson. I know that I've lived in Raven Brooks—quite possibly the weirdest town on Earth—for about six months, and we wouldn't live here at all except that we had to leave Germany in a hurry, and Dad's parents conveniently left him their house in their will. I am positive that I don't know the whole story about why we had to leave Germany, and most of me is afraid to know. And I am 100 percent certain that the tunnels running under the weather station where my grandparents used to work is merely one squirming, slimy worm in a whole can I've managed to open,

More than anything, I am crystal clear on this one fact: Now is *not* the time to spill the entire can. Now is the time to squeeze the lid back on. Shut it tight. Pretend I don't even know there's a lid or a can in the first place.

"Tunnels? Who said anything about . . . ahhhh, my head," I say, pushing my palm to my forehead and squinting against the pain. "What were you guys saying about a fall?"

I don't dare open my eyes to see if it's working. I wait for the silence to subside. To my relief, it does.

"You fell out of a tree," Dad says, his voice softening to the concern he expressed when he first rushed into the room.

"A tree?"

Dad chuckles. "Surprised? Me, too. You were never much of a climber."

I let myself laugh a little, too, wondering if he knows I'm playing dumb.

"I don't understand . . . What was I doing? . . . Where was . . . ?"

"In the woods, during the Unveiling Ceremony," Dad says, his face darkening a little.

Right. Because I was supposed to meet my family there after the imaginary project I was working on with Trinity beforehand.

My face flushes hot. "Sorry," I say, and I'm not sure if I'm apologizing for lying, or for not being there for his big moment, or for ruining the big moment when apparently I came crashing to the ground after inexplicably climbing a tree.

Dad clears his throat. I pretend that means "I forgive you."

Only after I look down at my hands in shame do I see the little dirt crescents underneath my fingernails. A long splinter embedded deep into my palm has turned the flesh around it pink.

In one crushing glance, the entire memory comes flooding back.

I'm running through the tunnels. But someone else is running, too. Chasing me.

No, not chasing me. I'm chasing *them.*

The footsteps grow louder as I close the gap between us. I crash through the tunnel, taking turns blindly as I push my fear aside. There's something in my hand, something smooth and flat and folded. It's Mr. Gershowitz's wallet.

Panting, I stop to listen for the footsteps and find them farther ahead now. I sprint to catch up and, slowly, a sweet, familiar smell begins to fill the air. All of a sudden, I'm pushing through a heavy metal door and ducking under pipes and vats and tripping over cables. A safety bulletin posted to the wall flaps beside me as I rush past it, but I register the Golden Apple Corporation logo even in the dark of the basement. Yes, that's it—I'm underneath the Golden Apple factory.

Next thing I know, I'm standing in the doorway leading out of the basement and into the forest.

I look down again at my hands. Tucked inside the wallet is Mr. Gershowitz's blood-stained ID.

"Come back!" I try to yell to the person I'm chasing, but my throat is parched and hoarse. It's Mr. Gershowitz. I remember now.

I run after him, ducking past branches and dodging sharp twigs. The woods no longer look familiar; panic begins to take hold again as I venture deeper and deeper into the thick overgrowth.

With my lungs burning and my legs beginning to shake, I'm just about to give up when I hear the crack of a branch so close by. I thought I was chasing Mr. Gershowitz, but now that I'm nearly upon him, I start to wonder if it's really him I've been chasing.

There's a disturbance in the leaves no more than thirty feet from the tree I'm hiding behind.

I have to look. I've come all this way, and now I have to look.

I try to swallow away my panic, but that only fills my stomach with air. Inch by inch, I creep my head around the thick trunk of the tree.

I stop swallowing air and suddenly forget how to breathe. If I didn't know better, I'd say it isn't breathing, either. It's so still, it could be a statue. But this thing is no statue.

I cover my head to protect my eyes from flying debris.

The crows come next, seemingly thousands of them, screeching their way across the purple sky like a dark jet stream, bringing chaos to the air. By the time they pass, I can't hear the voices over the speakers anymore. I can't hear anything.

I peer around the tree, but it's gone. The only evidence anything had been there at all is a broken branch from the tree above.

In that tree above is a nest that's somehow big enough for a human.

I'm climbing the tree before I know what I'm doing. I'm climbing, even though it's a horrible idea. I'm climbing faster than I've ever climbed in my entire life. I'm climbing, even though I am not nearly coordinated or strong enough to lift myself through the high branches and into the nest that until now has been little more than fable.

This is it, *I think.* This is where I'll find some answers.

Then, without even a creak as a warning, the branch under my left foot gives way. I manage one undignified scream before the world goes dark.

"Aaron?"

Dad is crouched beside the bed now, a deep crease folding his forehead in half. He almost looks . . . no, he *does* look worried.

"It's . . . it's just been a hard day, I guess," I say.

Dad nods but doesn't unfold his brow. It's one of those moments when the real Dad is here, the one who used to show me his blueprints before anyone else, even Mom, telling me not to tell Mya or she'd get jealous. The dad who tells me I'm capable of great things.

This is the Dad I used to be able to tell everything to. He would listen, even though he'd get that scary angry face. He'd hear me all the way out before grounding me, and even then, I'd know it would just be to keep me safe.

I don't tell him, though. I don't know why, but something about that day in the tunnels—the creature in the forest and Mr. Gershowitz's wallet and all the rest—tells me to keep it to myself, at least for now. At least until my head clears.

"Go to sleep," Dad says. "I'll stay until you do."

He does stay. I know because just as I fade into the blissful

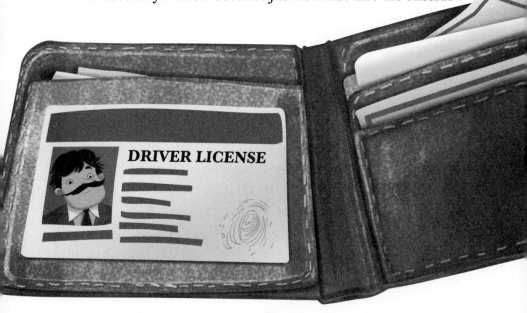

dark again, I hear the slow, steady breath of the dad I don't know as well, the one who took us out of Germany and brought us here. He's the one whose breath moves in and out of his lungs methodically, as methodically and secretively as his thoughts. The last thing I see before closing my eyes is the fold in his brow disappearing.

* * *

"Mom, I can't breathe."

"Ease up, Diane. He doesn't need a fractured rib on top of everything."

"What were you doing up there?" Mom says, holding me by the shoulders before pulling me in. I hear my back crack.

"What on earth were you thinking?"

"Mom—"

"Diane, for heaven's sake."

"I'm sorry, I'm sorry. I know what you need. A bath. A nice, warm bath," Mom says, smoothing her hands over the front of her pants as she tries to collect herself. I haven't even moved out of the foyer yet. I'm still wearing my hospital bracelet.

"A bath? I'm not a toddler, Mo—"

She spins on her heel and gives me a look, so I know it's this or more scolding.

A bath it is.

"I'll go get some scissors for that thing," Dad says, nodding at my plastic bracelet.

Only then do I see Mya lurking near the corner of the living room, staring a hole into my chest. She doesn't say anything.

Mya's never quiet, so this strikes me as strange, but then I remember Unveiling Day, and the lies I told to go to the weather station, and the trust I didn't show her or anyone else. *You know what,* I think, *maybe Mya is justified. This time.*

"Look, Mya, it wasn't personal, okay? It was just something I needed to do on my own."

She isn't interested, though. She's halfway up the stairs to her bedroom before I can even finish my sentence.

"Mya, c'mon," I try, but it's no use. I could keep trying to convince her, to make her understand that I was only trying to protect her from the awful truth about our family. It was bad enough I might discover that our grandparents were almost definitely the ones who started the fire at the Golden Apple factory all those years ago.

I could try to convince her that I was only doing what I thought was best. If I'm being totally honest, though, I wasn't thinking about her in that moment, except to consider that she might slow me down. Maybe, if I'm being completely truthful, I wanted the truth all for myself so I could decide what to do with it.

I lie in bed for a long time that night, unable to sleep in my own room after having spent the last several nights in the hospital. I never thought I'd miss the sound of those beeping machines and the nurses' calls to one another down the hall. The house is so quiet, I'm unnerved.

Too much silence is bad for me. It just gives me more time to think—about how Mya's mad at me, about how my grandparents burned down an entire factory, about Germany and the way we left it. I stare at the sketchpad and charcoal on my desk and try to convince myself to get up and draw, but just as I'm about to climb down from my bunk, I hear the tiny padding of Mya's footsteps down the hall.

Mya. I hop down and quietly peek my head out the door, but I don't see her.

As quietly as I can, I creep to the top of the landing and strain my ears for some sign of where she went. Then, faint but certain in the still air of the house, I hear the basement door open and close.

A tinge of bitterness creeps to the corners of my mouth, and I bite down against the thought that she might be going to *my* spot—the small, windowless room in the basement that's been my drawing spot since the first day we moved into this house. What, so I stayed a few nights at the hospital and now I'm chopped liver?

"Be mad all you want," I grumble to myself, inching down the stairs in socked feet. "But do it somewhere else, Mouse. That's *my* room."

I've barely reached the bottom step when Mom pops out of nowhere.

"You're on bedrest," she says. It might be dark, but I can still see her scowling.

This might be the same woman who made me take a bath earlier this evening, but Mom's not *that* soft. I know when I've crept up to her limit.

"But Mya—" I try feebly.

"Mya has nothing to do with this," she says, cutting me off. "Bed."

"But—"

"BED."

I am no match for Mom. She's not entirely wrong, either; my head is starting to pound again.

I drag myself up the stairs, Mom following behind me.

Back in my room, I slide my sketchpad and charcoal from the desk and climb into bed, tenting the covers over me with a flashlight. I try to push away the thought of my basement hideaway being usurped right at this very moment.

Instead, I squint against the throbbing behind my eyes and press the smoky lead to the paper, tracing lines and smudging shadows into the shape of the very last thing I remember seeing before I climbed that tree.

Feathers, shining and black and crested at the back.

A head, narrowed to a sharp black beak.

A hunched form, as tall as a full-grown adult.

A Forest Protector.

Chapter 2

"**D**id you fall because of the crows, or did a branch break, or—"

"Is it a concussion?"

"Do you have amnesia?"

"How many fingers am I holding up?"

"Why'd your dad think we were working on a project?"

"What project? Did I miss something? It's not for history, is it? I can't lose any more points in history."

"You GUYS!"

Four sets of wide eyes stare at me like I'm some sort of alien. It's just my friends, but suddenly *I do* feel like an alien.

"You're right," Trinity says, always the first one to turn rational. "Why don't you just start from the beginning."

Enzo, happy as usual to follow Trinity's lead, nods in agreement. "Take your time."

"But not too much time," says his sister, Maritza. "We've already been waiting for *days*."

Maritza is Mya's age, but she at least seems far more interested in hearing my side of things.

This moment feels like a moment I won't ever be able to

take back. If I divulge everything to my friends now, what will they think of my family? What will they think of Mya and me?

Hey, so, funny story, but remember how you were trying to convince me that my grandparents weren't actually arsonists bent on revenge against the richest family in town for yanking away their research funding? Well, ha ha, guess what? Turns out their office had a secret underground tunnel conveniently connected right to the very factory basement where a fire burned down the first Golden Apple factory. Isn't that the most hilarious thing you've ever heard?

Somehow, I don't see that going well.

"Okay, I changed my mind," Maritza says. "Don't take your time. I'm about to hit retirement age over here."

"You do like bingo," Enzo says.

"Just get on with it," Maritza says.

It's pointless. They're going to find out one way or another. If my friends and I have anything in common, it's nosiness.

So, I tell them about the passage in the wall and the tumble I took into the tunnel. I tell them about the broken lantern and the bloody wallet. I tell them about the person I chased who I thought was Mr. Gershowitz but who is also definitely *not* Mr. Gershowitz. I tell them about the nest.

When I finish, I enjoy the first moment of quiet all day. I only enjoy it for a minute, though.

"Hang on," says Enzo, getting there before everyone else for once. "That's why you were up in the tree? You saw one of the nests?"

"Yup."

"What was in it?"

Enzo is reaching critical mass.

"I didn't exactly get that far," I say, pointing to the bruise peeking out from my hairline.

"Right. Sorry."

Maritza shakes her head slowly. "I can't tell if you're incredibly brave or incredibly stupid."

"Stupid. Definitely stupid," says Mya, offering her first contribution of the day. She's been so quiet, I almost forgot she was there, too.

"Hang on," Trinity says, staring at the carpet like it's worrying her. "You found Mr. Gershowitz's wallet?"

I nod again, but this time, something in my stomach bobs up and down. I push away the memory of that smear of blood.

"Where is it now?" she asks. "The wallet, I mean."

The thing in my stomach drops like an anvil. How could it not have occurred to me until now? The wallet—the only sign of Mr. Gershowitz for months—and here I am in possession of it.

Except I'm not, because it wasn't in the hospital when I woke up. I would have remembered. Someone would have seen it.

Unless . . .

I'm suddenly back in the hospital bed, or the memory of it anyway, my head pounding and my questions spilling out of my mouth, and there's Dad, looming over me, warning me to keep quiet about the wallet.

Dad couldn't have taken it, though. "What would even be the purpose of that?" I mutter to myself.

"Purpose of what?" Mya asks, eyeing me suspiciously.

I look at her, betrayal still stiffening her jaw, and I can almost convince myself she knows what I'm thinking.

But she couldn't because you haven't bothered to tell her anything.

"Aaron," Enzo says, slowly waving a hand in front of my face.

"Huh?"

"The wallet?" he says, tipping his head to the side. "You need me to call your dad or something? You look a little pale."

"No!" I blurt at the mention of my dad, then quickly recover. "I mean, nah, I'm fine. Just tired, I guess."

They're staring at me again.

"Where's the wallet, dummy?" Mya asks, sighing impatiently.

"Oh, uh, I . . ."

It's weird. What reason would Dad have to take the wallet?

"I guess it's still in the tunnel."

Maritza shakes her head. "But I thought you said you ran out with it."

I shrug. "I thought I did, but who knows? Maybe I dropped it under the tree when I tried to climb to the nest. It's kind of hard to remember with a head injury."

Maritza and Enzo exchange a look.

"No way. First sign of Mr. Gershowitz since he went missing? The press would've picked up on that for sure," says Maritza.

There's that feeling in my stomach again.

"The press?"

Because that's what this situation is missing: more attention.

"Relax," Enzo says, dropping a hand on my shoulder. "Your secrets are safe with us. You've got a guy on the inside now."

Enzo puffs his chest out a little, and I see Trinity stifle a giggle out of the corner of my eye.

"'On the inside'?" I ask. "So what, you have, like, blood ties now or something?"

Enzo brushes me off. "You're looking at the *Raven Brooks Banner*'s official junior correspondent in charge of community content."

"He's even got his own desk at the *Banner* office," Trinity says, and I swear I see Enzo grow another inch.

"They probably just want another reporter on the ground, and they know they don't have to pay me. *Channel Four News* keeps scooping Golden Apple stories from us, and it's starting to rile Dad up in a big way."

"And he's going to write a story about the Young Inventors Club!" Maritza chimes in.

"Maritza, I've told you a million times already—"

"Yeah, yeah, I know, you're a very serious journalist, blah blah. Just put our picture in the paper. I'm not asking a lot. We're totally official. Look!" she says, sticking her wrist in Enzo's face. A gold-colored charm bracelet with one shiny golden apple dangles from the link. "We even have bracelets!"

Mya holds up her arm to reveal her matching charm. "And one for Lucy."

"For sure, we're going to have to make more," Maritza says to Mya, who nods earnestly.

"Riiiiight," Enzo says like only a big brother could. I know this trick well. "Because people will be lining up to join your little dork club."

Maritza shrugs. "We'll even do the interview for free!"

Enzo looks genuinely offended. "You're asking me to compromise my journalistic integrity, and frankly I'm surprised by you, Maritza. Of all people, my own sister should know me better."

Maritza isn't listening, though. She and Trinity are too busy stifling their laughter to even attempt to take him seriously.

I'm taking him seriously, though.

"Hang on, just how much of what I've told you is already out there?" I ask, swirling my hand in the air like maybe I could catch all the secrets floating around. I have this absurd image of me holding a butterfly net, swiping at ghosts in the atmosphere.

Enzo just smiles. "I told you, I've got you covered."

My head is starting to ache again. "And I appreciate that. I do. I just have absolutely no idea what that means."

"It means his 'journalistic integrity' only applies to his sister," Maritza says, souring.

"He wrote about something else instead," Trinity says, more diplomatically. "About the Golden Apple flavors that'll be featured at the park."

"Spoiler alert: It's all of them," Maritza says, side-eyeing Enzo.

Enzo shrugs. "People like feel-good stories. Nobody wants to read about some kid falling out of a tree and cracking his head and not dying. No offense."

"None taken," I say, and it's true. I'm too busy feeling relieved to feel the sting of irrelevance. The less people are talking about my nosedive in the forest, the fewer questions I'll have to answer about why I was in the tree in the first place.

"Check it out," Enzo says, digging a folded newsprint from his pocket and spreading it out before me like a treasure map.

There, in all its newsworthy brilliance, is a bold headline:

And there, underneath the headline, is Enzo Esposito's author photo. Maritza has nothing to worry about in the competition for biggest dork. Enzo looks like he's just been asked to sing the national anthem at the Super Bowl wearing a llama costume.

"You look great," I say.

Enzo beams.

For the first time since waking up in the hospital, I'm starting to feel like everything might just be okay—or at least, the Peterson family's unique brand of okay—when shouting erupts from downstairs in the form of my dad's baritone voice. He's not speaking to *me*, thankfully. But he is speaking to *someone*. I can't help but listen. We tiptoe out of my room and hang over the landing, hoping Dad doesn't notice our shadows from above.

"If I thought you had even half a sense of humor, I'd ask if you were kidding me!" Dad roars.

Nobody says a word.

"My own son only just got out of the hospital, there's already been one accident onsite with a worker, and you want *'to speed things up'*?"

Mya and I look at each other. We don't even mean to. It's just habit. *Did you know about that? What does it mean? Who's Dad on the phone with?* Even when we're mad at each other, it's like there's some sort of brother-sister portal between our brains that can never close.

"No, *you* listen to *me*! I don't care what your deadline is . . ."

There's a pause.

"The beginning of summer? Are you out of your mind?"

Dad's pacing the floor as far as the phone cord in the living room will let him. The coil is already wrapped around his shoulders in a double loop.

"Who do you think he's talking to?" Trinity whispers.

"If you think just because you're the new mayor, or because you're a Tavish, you can intimidate me, you—"

"Well, I guess that answers that," Maritza says, but she must have said it a little too loudly, because all at once, Dad's roar grinds to a halt, and his ire is redirected at the very landing we're standing on.

"*Retreat!*" Enzo hisses, and we collectively flee to my room, as though there is any chance in the world he didn't see a flock of five nosy kids gaping at him from the staircase.

Not two seconds later, a soft knock precedes my mom's face through a crack in my bedroom door.

"I think maybe it's time to call it a day, kids," she says, and her forced calm is fooling no one.

"Bye!" Maritza whispers to me, but she barely has a chance to wave before Trinity has pulled her through the door.

"See you soon, man," Enzo says, but he might as well be saying, "See you soon so long as it's not at your house." I can't really blame him.

I can hear Mom escorting them past the storm swirling through the living room, sending them cheerily on their way with a "Thanks for stopping by!" before swinging the front door shut.

Sometime during the mass exodus, Mya drifted away, too, leaving me to listen to the incensed echoes of my dad's futile protests. I creep back to the landing and crouch behind the wall just out of sight. Dad's losing whatever battle he's fighting—that much is clear. And while I'm comforted by hearing him be so protective of me, I can't seem to focus on that part. What was that he said about an accident at the building site? I've seen Dad stressed before, but this is a different kind of freak-out.

It's the next thing he says, though, that I know right away is going to keep me up the whole night.

"What exactly are you accusing me of, Tavish?"

His voice is so quiet, I think maybe I didn't hear him correctly. Now he's completely silent, staring into the dark corner of the living room while he presses his ear against the receiver. His face doesn't move. He doesn't even blink.

Then the strangest thing happens. Dad gives up.

"Yes," he says after the longest silence. Then again, "Yes."

Another long silence passes, and Dad closes his eyes against the dark corner he was staring at.

The last thing he says before he carefully places the receiver back in its cradle is: "I understand."

Mom is at the other end of the room, and if I had to guess, I'd say my face looks a lot like hers—puckered around all the worry places, pale, tired.

"Ted, what'd he say?" she asks quietly.

Dad walks past her.

"Ted?"

Mom probably knows better than to follow Dad. He's headed down the hallway to his study, and I should know better, too. I know I should leave him alone.

But the way he just gave up, the way he agreed to whatever ludicrous deadline Mayor Tavish insisted on, it all happened after he accused my dad of something . . . but what?

"Dad? Dad!"

I chase him like a puppy, nipping at his heels as he rounds the corner down the back hallway.

"Not now, Aaron," he says in the same resigned tone he used with the mayor.

But there's something I need to know. I won't be able to sleep tonight unless I at least ask.

"Dad, do you know what happened to Mr. Gershowitz?"

He stops cold, and I have to swerve so I don't crash into him.

He doesn't turn around, though. He stands stone still, his back rigid, his shoulders blocking most of the light in the hallway.

I already know I've made a terrible mistake.

He's quiet for so long, I consider creeping away and slinking up the stairs. It'll be like I never said a thing.

Before I have a chance, with his back still to me, he says, "Of course I don't."

He sounds different than I've ever heard him sound before. His body is so big, yet his voice is suddenly small.

He sounds hurt.

"Dad, I'm—"

I'm sorry. That's what I mean to say. I want to tell him I'm sorry for even asking. But the hurt in his voice disappears as fast as it arrived, and he says more sternly, "That's enough questions about Ike Gershowitz. Understood?"

He still hasn't turned around, and I can't decide if that's a good or a bad thing.

"Okay," I say, even though it's not. It's the furthest thing from okay. "But I—"

"Not another word!" he roars, swiveling on his heel to face me for the first time in the hallway.

I jump back hard enough to clip my heel on the baseboard.

All I can do is muster the courage to nod.

Then he turns and storms down the hall, grumbling something about privacy and his study and being better off in the basement.

I don't dare move until he slams his study door behind him.

Mom's hand on my shoulders makes me jump again, and I'm not sure how much more my heart can take tonight.

"Bed," she whispers, squeezing my shoulder, and I wish it comforted me the way she means for it to, but it doesn't. The questions follow me to bed that night and keep me up until the night sky gives way to dusk.

What is my dad hiding?

Chapter 3

When school break comes to a close, Mya still holds a grudge against me. Sure, there were moments of the old Mya here and there, like on Easter, when she let me have the last sausage at breakfast, or later that night, when I gave her a drawing, but since falling out of the tree, not a day has passed since then that she hasn't reminded me of the way I cut her out of my search for the truth about our family.

To be honest, I'm starting to feel less and less sorry.

We're walking on our way to school when we're hit with a bad rainstorm. Mya had thought it would rain because she saw the crows leave. I didn't. I told her not to take an umbrella. I guess we both lose.

"Sorry, Mouse," I say, covering my head with my hands.

She glares at me from under her hood. "You stink at apologies."

"That's because I didn't mean it."

"What?" she yells over the wind.

"I said I've never seen it rain like this!" I shout.

* * *

"An incongruous weather anomaly," Mrs. Ryland says, slapping the chalk against the board as she writes the words.

It's sixth period, and only now are my feet starting to feel dry.

"Researchers have been studying the phenomena for decades here in Raven Brooks. Our isolated weather events are something of a legend in the region!"

"Hear that, Seth? You could be a weather celebrity!"

Seth Jenkins hops to his feet on cue while Ruben Smith circles his desk with an imaginary camera.

"Oooh, that's great! Now show me 'snow'! Love it! Now look 'stormy'!"

Seth strikes pose after pose while most of the class snickers. Mrs. Ryland seems to have learned by now that the best thing is to wait for the Seth and Ruben Show to play itself out. Most of the kids get sick of them faster than she could make them be quiet.

Seth snorts and sits back down. "Nerds. Who gets excited about weather anyway?"

Literally the entire class turns to the poster of a tornado that's been prominently displayed in Mrs. Ryland's class all year. It says in huge block letters WEATHER REALLY BLOWS ME AWAY!

Mrs. Ryland is only slightly fazed.

"Mr. Jenkins, I can make you a detention celebrity if you'd prefer."

Seth sinks into his seat and scowls.

Mrs. Ryland continues, "As junior meteorologists, how might we get to the root of these anomalous events?"

Crickets.

"Anyone?"

Nope. No one.

Mrs. Ryland sighs. "We've only been talking about it all school year," she says, finally looking defeated.

More silence, but now with a tinge of guilt.

"We begin with a *hypothesis*," she says, exaggerating the word.

Grumbles of recognition. Right, hypothesis. Because we woke up every morning of break and thought of the word *hypothesis*.

"I have a hypothesis," Enzo pipes up.

In a happy turn of events—I guess the universe decided I needed a modicum of a break at the end of last term— Enzo was transferred into sixth-period geography with me. I suppose it might have had something to do with the highly predictable nervous breakdown of Mr. Delvy, the ancient history teacher (not a teacher of ancient history, mind you, but a teacher of advanced years).

It's a pretty funny story actually. He threw a bust of Alexander Hamilton through a window and that was that. The school district must have decided that one term of history was adequate, and the kids were farmed out to different sixth-period classes. I was lucky to get Enzo in mine.

"Mr. Esposito, that's lovely!" Mrs. Ryland says, and she means it because to her, weather is indeed lovely.

"I think it all goes back to the crows."

My happiness to have Enzo in my class fades a tad. Again with the crows. Are he and my sister swapping bird conspiracy theories?

"Interesting," Mrs. Ryland says. "Go on."

"Yes, Enzo, do go on," Seth Jenkins says, propping his chin in his hand and feigning interest. "Been spending some quality time with the birds, have we?"

Enzo plucks a leaf from Seth's head that's gotten trapped in his gelled spikes.

"Dude, Seth, you're like a Forest Protector?" Ruben asks, cackling.

"Man, shut up," grumbles Seth.

"My cousin's best friend's brother saw one over the break! It was practically in his backyard!" some kid pipes up from the back.

"My uncle swears there was one hiding in a tree outside his work!" someone else says.

"Like three different people on my block said they found a nest, but when they went back to look for it, it was gone!" says yet another kid.

"Okay, okay," Mrs. Ryland yells over the class, but I can tell she's just as excited as the rest of them. She may or may not have a pen on her desk that she says is a quill, but it's long and shiny and black and looks a heck of a lot like other long black feathers I'd rather not remember finding recently.

"I think we're all familiar with the Forest Protector urban legend, and for those who aren't, I'm sure you'll have no trouble getting someone in town to tell you a story," she says. "I believe we've rudely interrupted Mr. Esposito."

Mrs. Ryland turns back to Enzo. "Please, continue with your hypothesis."

"Well," says Enzo, "it does kind of have to do with the Forest Protectors, or at least the crows. There seems to be some kind of correlation between the flock of crows—"

"Murder," Mrs. Ryland says, a wicked glint in her eye.

"Um, what?" says Enzo, clearly rattled. He's not the only one.

"A murder of crows," Mrs. Ryland says. "That's what a group is called."

I wish she'd stop saying "murder." I also wish my brain would stop conjuring the image of Mr. Gershowitz's blood-smeared wallet when she does.

"Oh," says Enzo. "Okay. So anyway, the birds act all strange, and then the sky turns that funny purple color, and then poof! Weather weirdness."

Out of nowhere, Mrs. Ryland turns to me. "Mr. Peterson, as you know, your grandparents were considered industry pioneers in their research. I don't suppose they ever mentioned any of their . . . ah . . . unique findings to you?"

Her eyes are doing this twinkling thing that's making me uncomfortable. It's like she's really hungry, but for intel.

Of course, it could just be her mention of my grandparents that's making me want to bolt from the classroom and maybe just never come back.

"I never met them," I say flatly.

The twinkle extinguishes.

"I see."

"Actually," Enzo says, swooping in, "my research at the *Banner* shows that there are stories of crow sightings and, er, sightings of other things, dating back to at least the 1960s, maybe even earlier."

Mrs. Ryland's focus shifts back to Enzo. "Ah, yes, I seem to recall there being an enthusiastic young reporter working there at the time. Nathaniel something or the other. He was very keen on the crow stories. I suppose that's why he was let go."

"Let go?" Enzo asks.

Mrs. Ryland shrugs. "Pity, too. He apparently died in an unfortunate accident not long after that, or so I heard."

"Whoa, what kind of accident?" Seth asks, finally interested. "Did he, like, get hit by a train or something?"

"Ooh, or crushed by a steamroller!" Ruben posits.

"Dude, what if he fell into one of those big newspaper printing thingies and got squeezed through the wheels? Oh man, all his guts just squishing through—"

"I think we all get the picture, Mr. Jenkins," Mrs. Ryland says, stepping in way too late.

"Mrs. Ryland, can you please tell Seth and Ruben that they're disgusting pigs?" a girl from the middle row says.

"Mrs. Ryland, can you please tell Megan Lipsey her hair tie looks like a giant swirly turd on top of her head?" Ruben shoots back.

Megan scoffs. "It's a *scrunchie!*" she says.

"Enough!" Mrs. Ryland yells.

Through the battle royal of sixth period, Enzo scoots his desk a little closer to mine.

"Have you ever heard about that reporter dying?" he whispers to me.

"Um, you mean back in the sixties? Enzo, this might come as a shock to you, but I wasn't alive back then."

"But has your dad ever mentioned anything like that?"

"Until this summer, I didn't even know the town of Raven Brooks existed. You might have noticed my dad isn't exactly the sharing type. Honestly, I can't even imagine him as a kid."

Enzo doesn't argue.

"Anyway, why does it matter?" I ask.

"Look, it's not my fault you're wearing poop in your head," says Ruben.

"*No one* is wearing bodily waste on *anything*!" Mrs. Ryland yells.

Enzo leans closer.

"I've been through those old archives a million times looking for stories related to all this weirdness—the weather, the Forest Protectors, your grandparents."

"Okay?" I say.

"Norman Darby—that was the name of the reporter who wrote all those stories. He suddenly stopped, or at least as far as I could find."

"Yeah, because he died, right?"

I nod to the general chaos in the room as a reminder of how all this started—with speculation on Mr. Darby's untimely death.

"What if it, you know, it wasn't an accident?" Enzo says, eyes wide.

"So, what, you think he got squished in the printer?" I say, begging him to be kidding.

"C'mon, gimme a little more credit than that," Enzo replies, glancing back at Seth and Ruben. "But don't you think it's a little weird that in a newspaper where every minute something is reported, there wasn't a *single* story about the death of one of the *Banner*'s former employees?"

Enzo takes a breath, letting it all sink in for me.

"It really makes you wonder if Norman stumbled onto something he wasn't supposed to know," he says. As if I wasn't thinking that already.

* * *

That night, I know what I have to do. I have to speak with Mya.

Mya is my closest ally, and with all that's going on, I guess I need her more than I realized.

I knock on her bedroom door once, more of a warning that I'm coming in rather than permission. I find her sitting on her bed, crisscross applesauce, with a bunch of papers splayed out around her.

I don't have time to ask Mya what the papers are there for. I need to get to the bottom of this.

"Mya, you need to get over whatever grudge you hold against me," I say.

Mya whips around, her eyes aflame. But her expression looks calm—aloof. I never thought Mya and Dad looked alike until now. From where I am, standing at the threshold of her bedroom, I finally see it, that Peterson glare—it's in the way they arch their eyebrows and jut their lips, and you wonder what's really going on in their brains. I wonder if this expression comes naturally to Mya or if maybe she practiced it in our bathroom mirror. She's probably been waiting for this moment since the millisecond I got home from the hospital.

Mya sighs, looking back down at the papers in front of her.

"You've run out of people to talk to," she says flatly.

I squint my eyes and try to see what's so important that Mya won't look back up from it, but all I can make out is the ink from her purple gel pen among dozens of loose-leaf papers scattered about.

"You just want me to get over my grudge because you want to talk to someone, and no one else is around," Mya continues. "You were all twitchy at dinner. You have a secret, and you want to tell me, and you want me to care, but I don't."

"I wasn't twitchy," I say defensively.

"I don't care about your secret," Mya says in a tone that means *business*.

"Now I know you're lying," I reply. "You always care about secrets."

Mya shrugs. "Not this time."

This nonchalant Mya is really throwing me for a loop. Where's the nagging little sister I know and despise?

"Mya, knock it off. You're overreacting."

"I'm not reacting at all."

Well, she's got me there.

"I was just trying to protect you, okay?"

"Nice try," she says, and honestly, that stings a little.

"I was!"

"No, you were being greedy. You were trying to make yourself feel important by finding out the truth first. You weren't thinking about me or anyone else. Even though I'm just as afraid of the secrets as you are," she says.

I'm left to sit in the quiet while a heavy load sinks into my brain. It hurts, because Mya's right.

"You didn't trust me," she says, driving the point through my stomach. "Even though there's no one else in the world in the same situation as you. And you shut me out."

I want badly for her to be wrong so I can walk back to my room in a huff and vow to keep our family's secrets tucked away so they can't hurt anyone, and put the lid on this all, here and now.

But that would mean pushing Mya away—*Mya*, who is the only one who could *actually* understand.

"Okay," I say. It's all I can manage in the moment because I'm just so dumbfounded, I'm not sure if anything else will suffice.

It seems to be enough, though, because after another minute or so of staring me down, the flame in Mya's eyes extinguishes, and she shoves her papers and pens aside so I can sit on her bed and spill.

In a matter of minutes, I tell Mya everything, The chase, the man, the bird, the nest. Dad's reaction at the hospital. What Enzo found (or rather *didn't* find) in the *Banner*'s archives. Throughout it all, I notice that there are dark circles under Mya's eyes. They definitely weren't there before. I guess I've been so in my head, I haven't noticed if she's been sleeping or not.

We're just about to talk about our grandparents when the door bursts open and a pool of light spills in from the hallway, flanked by Mom, who waltzes in holding her electric toothbrush.

"I see you two have worked things out," Mom says.

"Mom," Mya says, annoyed.

"Sorry," Mom replies, holding her hands up in surrender. "I'll knock next time. But I heard voices while I was brushing my teeth, and it's late, and I think it's time for you two to call it a night."

I fully expect Mya to protest, but what happens next *truly* surprises me. Mya nods with the maturity of a thirty-year-old who has to go to work in the morning. She surrenders, just like that.

Before I'm able to process all of this, Mom shoos me out of the room and tucks me in. I wonder if she's cocooned me around the pillows to help me sleep better—or to stop me from getting up. Just as I'm about to think about what Mom's hiding from me, I'm asleep, away from all of this, in dreamland doing dream things.

And then I feel a tug on my feet.

"Yowww!" I gasp.

"Shhh!" says a silhouette. I yank my eyes open and recognize the silhouette is Mya. It's three thirty in the morning. Has Mya slept? What's going on? I wonder if I'm still dreaming when Mya tiptoes out of my bedroom all stealth-like and gestures me to follow.

And, well, who am I to refuse?

I know where we're going the minute we hit the first staircase. Mom's done a really good job since I've gotten back from the hospital about making sure I don't "strain myself" (her words) by going to the basement. My heart does a little leap at the realization that I'll finally see whatever it is that's been going on down there. I cross my fingers and hope Mom doesn't poke out of her room to find me going to the one place she's been so keen on keeping me away from.

When Mya opens the door to the basement, my heart goes from leaping to sinking. It isn't my special sanctuary anymore.

* * *

The small square of concrete is no longer littered with my pencils and sketchpads. They've been stacked neatly in a single dark corner. In no time at all, this place has turned a murky shade of gray.

I guess I'm too busy slipping into that melancholy place to notice that Mya isn't in there with me anymore.

I spin toward the staircase, half expecting to see her flee-ing up the stairs and shutting the door behind her, locking me in for revenge. But there's no sign of Mya at all, just the dim light from the hallway emerging under the crack.

"Mya?" I whisper. No luck.

"Mya?" I try again, a little louder. "My—?"

"Would you keep up?" scolds a voice, and from the shadows emerges my little sister, acting like the older one, pulling me by my wrist into the darkest corner of the room.

And through a doorway.

"Hang on. Hang on!"

I walk back into the more familiar space, then through the doorway, then repeat the motion again.

"Yeah, yeah, there's a door," she says, old news to her.

"How . . . how could you not tell me you found this?" I squeak out before I realize it.

"Seriously?" she says, peering at me through the dark. There go those laser eyes of hers again.

"Fine," I say, "I guess I deserve that. But, Mya, this is huge! It's like . . . it's like a whole other world!"

"You haven't seen anything yet," she says, and the first spark of glee returns to her voice. I can't deny that I'm happy to hear it. It's undeniably *Mya*.

She starts to walk ahead before I stop her.

"Wait, how did I never see this? I thought I knew every inch of this basement!"

Without a word, Mya walks back to the cement square, stands beside the doorway, and presses a spot on the wall no one in their right mind would think is a button. If anything, it looks like a flaw in the plaster slathered over the concrete.

I shake my head in disbelief. Or wonder. Or admiration. I really don't know.

"Do I even want to know how you found it?" I ask, knowing there's at least a 50 percent chance she got here by snooping.

"The old-fashioned way," she says slyly, then disappears again through the doorway.

Yup. Snooping.

The hallway, if you can even call it that, could be twenty feet long or two hundred feet for all I know. It's so dark, I can't see the end of it, and as I keep my arm extended so I can at least feel the wind at Mya's back while she moves, I can't help but wonder at how scared she must have been while she was first exploring this forgotten depth of the house. I wasn't there to help her feel brave.

Then there's a small voice in the back of my head. *She didn't need me there to be brave.*

"Just a little farther," Mya says, no longer whispering but still keeping her voice low, as though not to disturb the quiet.

When we do eventually turn a corner, Mya stops short, and I rock onto my tiptoes to keep from running into her.

I hear a knob turn, a door creak, and a familiar smell immediately washes over me.

Old wood.

Time-worn paper.

Mustache wax.

Mya flicks a light switch, and a yellow glow pours from the lamp on the giant wooden desk covered in curled paper.

It's Dad's office. Except . . .

"Dad's office is upstairs," I say, though clearly it is not.

"He moved it," replies Mya. "He's been keeping the door upstairs locked to make us think he still uses it."

"I mean, he's been saying he's going to move down here forever, but I . . ."

I can't seem to finish a single thought.

"Didn't know this existed?" Mya says, filling in the blank.

"I guess I figured he meant the other spot in the basement," I say.

My spot. Or what *was* my spot.

As I scan the room, I keep coming back to the giant desk piled high with blueprints. I make it halfway across the room toward the desk when Mya beckons me to a space in the corner by a dusty bookshelf.

"You're gonna want to see this," she says, and once I'm beside her, she starts to walk away.

"Stay there," she says, and I watch as she returns to the doorway, and then, on another place in the wall that looks like a crack in the plaster, she presses what turns out to be a button, which releases a small handle of some sort, like a lever you'd pull in the event of an emergency.

Mya pulls the lever, but nothing could have prepared me for what happens next.

The smell hits me first, then the echo of dank walls surrounding moldy ground and a low ceiling.

All at once, I'm back in the tunnel system connecting the weather station to the Golden Apple factory.

And apparently, connecting my own house to those same places.

"You've got to be kidding me," I say.

"Yeah, funny, right?" Mya says, standing beside me again although she's definitely not laughing.

"This can't be real."

"Why do you think Dad moved his office down here?" Mya says, though on some level, we both know.

Not only is there more of a chance that Dad knows something about Mr. Gershowitz's disappearance, but it's also practically undeniable that our grandparents set the fire that burned down the Tavishes' factory.

"I don't know where it leads," Mya continues. "I haven't . . . I haven't explored it yet."

I know what she's leaving out. She was waiting for me.

This whole time, she wasn't holding a grudge because of *my* secret. She was mad she couldn't tell me *hers*.

"Mya," I say, steadying my voice. "I have to tell you something."

I take a deep breath.

"I didn't leave Mr. Gershowitz's wallet in the tunnel," I say.

I feel her stare shift from the tunnel to me.

"I had it in my hand when I was climbing that tree. I had it when they brought me to the hospital. I'm 100 percent *sure.*"

I hear Mya swallow.

"The hospital staff must have taken it," she says finally, flatly. "Or the paramedics. Maybe they were trying to identify *you—*"

"Wouldn't we have heard about that by now? They would've figured it out pretty quick. Missing man's wallet found with blood on it."

We're quiet again, both staring into the silent tunnel.

"So, then the only other person who could have taken it . . ."

Mya doesn't need to say it. We both know.

Without another word, we both step away from the tunnel entrance. At some point, we will have to see where it goes. At some point, we'll need to open the lid and look through and figure out what is *really* happening.

But that some point isn't now.

Mya leaves my side for just a moment as she walks to the other end of the room.

Just as she grasps the lever to seal the tunnel, I think I hear the sound of shuffling echoing from the farthest end of the tunnel, too deep in the darkness to show me what it could be. When I'm back in my bed, safe and sound, I replay the noise in my head, again and again. Each time, I can't shake the feeling, this gut, deep, harrowing feeling. I think it was a scratch of talons on the ground.

Chapter 4

Months go by. Mya and I don't really talk about what we found—I mean, how can you? I think both of us have tried to squash it all deep down. Pretend it didn't happen. You know, anything but *this*.

We're outside now on a beautifully sunny day, right by the Golden Apple Amusement Park. Technically, Enzo is the only one with any reason to be here, what with his fancy-schmancy apprenticeship at the *Banner* or whatever. The rest of us have zero excuse.

"Do you think they'll build a better path to the park once the construction is done? Or are they just going to make people walk the Poison Ivy Trail to get there?" Enzo says, hopping over a perfectly fine plant. He's determined not to let a single leaf touch his skin.

"Maybe this'll be one of the attractions," I offer. "Like a haunted mansion, but instead of vampires popping out of coffins, it's evil leaves ruining your summer."

Mya chuckles.

"We need to find the lead site manager," Maritza says to Lucy and Mya. "That way, we can find out about the

materials they use for the rides."

"You know you're not fooling anyone, right?" Enzo says to his sister.

"I beg your pardon."

"I know what you're trying to do," Enzo says, holding his messenger bag a little closer to him as though he has a sacred duty to protect whatever's in there. Which is just a notebook and a pen. I already saw it.

"Actually, I think a feature on the Young Inventors Club would make a good story," Trinity says, pausing to check the focus on her camera. Maritza isn't the only one here with an ulterior motive. Supposedly, Enzo asked Trinity along because she's the only one whose parents have a nice enough camera to document the story.

Supposedly.

And supposedly, I'm here to look after Mya, but we all know I'm headed to the tree I fell out of.

"You're not going to find anything," Trinity says to me

gently while I hang back with her and hold the camera lens. "People were all over that area after you fell. Trust me, if there was a nest, someone would have noticed. Plus, it's been *months*."

I smirk. "I'd like to think they were more interested in the poor kid lying on the ground than what was hidden in the leaves above."

"Okay, then afterward," she says. "We couldn't have been the only ones wanting to know what you were doing up there."

I shrug. "Kids are dumb. We climb trees for no reason."

I'm trying to be casual about it all, but in this group, Trinity is the furthest one from dumb, and I feel like she's getting too close to the real reason I want to visit the tree.

"I guess I just need to be able to say I did everything I could," I say, and she looks at me.

"For Mr. Gershowitz?" she says. "Aaron, none of that is your fault. No one blames you for leaving the wallet in the tunnel. You don't even remember being taken to the hospital. None of us would have done anything different."

She's right at the cliff of the truth now, and I need to find a way to change the subject fast. I could really use Mya's help; she's the only one who knows what I'm actually doing, but she's so wrapped up in Young Inventors Club business, I can't get her attention.

Luckily, Trinity talks herself away from the edge.

"But I guess if I were in your place, I'd want to make

sure I didn't leave any stone unturned. Just . . . don't get your hopes up, okay?"

I nod. "Got it. I'll go in completely hopeless."

"There's not going to be a nest, Aaron. And there's not going to be anything you can bring to the police to make them believe you found what you found in the tunnel. Not after the doctor said your brain was scrambled. Not when you're just a kid."

I nod again, doing my best mopey, "I know you're right" impression.

Eventually, after three near misses with the poison ivy and two arguments over what flavors of Golden Apples they should sell in the park, we reach the part of the path where I diverged on Unveiling Day when I was chasing . . . whatever I was chasing.

"You're sure you want to do this alone?" Enzo says, and it's just now occurring to everyone but Trinity and me that it probably isn't the best idea to split up.

"I've already tried," Trinity says, shaking her head like I'm a lost cause. I suppose she's not entirely wrong.

"Just hurry up, okay?" Mya says, playing her part perfectly. She's staring me down, though, so I know she's worried, too.

"You *guys*, he's gonna be gone for like five seconds. Find tree. Look up. No nest. Boom, he's back with us," says Maritza, rolling her eyes so hard she bobs her head.

Then she starts walking toward the construction site, grumbling something about being boring, and Maritza is suddenly my new favorite person.

Mya casts one final look at me before stumbling to keep up with the rest. Once they've disappeared through the net of overgrowth, I turn and sprint toward the place where I fell.

I had my doubts about whether or not I'd be able to locate the spot. These woods are so tangled and thick, it's easy for everything to start looking the same, especially when you're running in a panic. But it's daylight now, and the shrubbery has grown over. The moment I set foot off the path and into the brush, the sound of crunching leaves and twigs brings it all back.

The tree I hid behind is right where I remember it, with its knotted trunk and reaching branches. I half expect to find my own shoe prints in the soft earth at its base, but vines have already obscured the ground underneath, and as always, the forest has taken over, concealing all its secrets.

I take a few breaths to steady my thumping heart before peering around the corner. It's only after I exhale hard that I realize I was half expecting to see the thing with the beaked hood and cloak of feathers. Feeling a little braver, I creep around the trunk and make my way to the tree where the nest had been. I'm actually surprised to find the broken branch still there, lying on the ground, a downy blanket of moss forming over it.

I look up because I have to. I know I won't see a nest; Trinity was right about that. But it's hard not to look, and sure enough, I find nothing more than a missing branch and a place high in the canopy where a nest could easily have rested out of sight from anyone not looking for it.

It's not the nest I'm here for, though.

I'm on my hands and knees before I consider how wet and muddy the ground is, still soft from the last storm. I can feel the dampness seeping through the knees of my jeans, but I don't care. I shove the branch aside and dig, registering the dirt caking my nails, just like I found them upon waking up in the hospital.

"C'mon, c'mon," I say, growing more frantic as I scoop aside damp leaves and spiny twigs. "Just be here. Please just be here."

But it's not. I kick every branch and fallen leaf, every pebble and rock and stone within a twenty-foot radius of the tree. It's not here.

Mr. Gershowitz's wallet isn't here.

Trinity was right; I *had* been holding out hope, but not about the nest. I'd been holding on to the possibility that I'd dropped the wallet when I fell, and in the commotion and all the people, it'd gotten buried under the brush.

I'd been holding out hope that my dad hadn't been the one to take it.

The list against my dad is growing longer and longer:

His fight with Mr. Gershowitz before he went missing.

The lost wallet.

His refusal to talk about his supposed closest friend.

His refusal to let *me* talk about him.

And yet, all hope isn't lost. The fact remains that despite all the arrows pointing his way, there's absolutely no proof that my dad is at fault. Whoever—*whatever*—I chased out of the tunnel on Unveiling Day is still the one most likely to know exactly what happened to Mr. Gershowitz.

Still, I can't shake the feeling that my dad knows something about it. Just how much—and why he's keeping it such a secret—is what gnaws at my brain.

Slumped against the tree, I try to gather the motivation to rejoin my friends at the construction site. I'm just about to turn around when a sudden breeze sets something nearby tapping.

It sounds like a bird at first, maybe pecking at some dead leaf on the ground. But when I follow the sound more closely, I see that it's actually not coming from the ground but from a sliver of bark peeled from the tree's trunk near its base. Snagged in the bark, half obscured by a pile of foliage, is a yellowed scrap of paper I recognize immediately.

"No way."

I carefully brush away the leaves and twigs to reveal a torn shred of paper that's clearly been ripped from one of the notebooks scattered across my grandparents' abandoned office in the weather station.

"What?" I breathe, at last finding conclusive proof that someone besides me was not only in the weather station but was near this tree, too.

The paper is soft from being left out here in the cold and damp for who knows how long, and while some of the writing in one of my grandparents' script is still recognizable, most of the words are smeared and faded with age or exposure. Not that it ever made much sense anyway. There are words like "electromagnetic" and "atypical properties" and "flight migration," with asterisks and arrows and double underlines that make it all feel very important, but I don't know what it all means. It's my grandparents' writing, though. There's no mistaking the flourishing on their lettering.

I carefully unfold the sheet the rest of the way, but whatever was left is gone now.

Or so I think.

A bit of ink rubs onto my finger, probably fresh off the rain that we just had. But this ink is different. It's darker, all caps, and slanted to the right, like it was written in a hurry.

It's a list of names. Or at least, it *was* a list of names. Now it's just a scrap of paper that comes frustratingly close to something that might be helpful but isn't.

"M. Tavish," I read. And beside his name, "Roger Gersh." But the rest is missing.

"Eleanor R" and a line through the letters "Ma."

And then there's one unmistakable name at the bottom, floating there without purpose or explanation or any conceivable reason for being there. "Peterson."

My head is starting to hurt trying to piece together what any of it could mean. I'm straining so hard that, at first, I don't even hear the scratching. Only when it suddenly stops do I register something behind me.

I spin on my heel fast, scanning the thick clumps of trees all around, but whatever was making the sound remains silent now.

Was it even there in the first place?

I hold my breath and squint through the trees without moving my head.

Suddenly, from the other side of me, another scratching, this one even closer.

Is it possible for something to sound sharp? Sharper than a fingernail? Sharp like a . . . talon?

But that's nuts, I tell myself. No bird could make a sound that loud.

Unless it's not a bird.

Another scratch followed by a heavy footfall.

It's just your imagination. You're remembering what you saw the last time you were here.

Another footfall. Another dragging scratch, this one closer than the rest.

I press my back against the same tree I hid behind after chasing who I thought was Mr. Gershowitz. A horrible déjà vu overtakes me.

"Get it together, Aaron," I say, forcing myself to take one deep breath after another. "This isn't the time."

I have to laugh at myself because really, when *is* it the time to lose your mind?

Hearing myself laugh when no one else is around only makes me sound more demented, though.

Suddenly, a twig snaps so close by, I jump to the side, hitting my head on the same tree.

Seriously, this thing is out to get me.

Paranoia rushes through me, and I'm locked in place as I fight the suspicion that I'm not imagining anything—that I'm not being followed.

I'm being hunted.

I've never run so fast in my life. Not when our landlord in Germany, Herr Schneider, caught me picking locks in the building. Not when I was trying to catch the bus on my first day in Raven Brooks. Not after I burst through the door of the Golden Apple factory in pursuit of a mystery I wish I'd never uncovered.

I run so fast, I don't feel the burning in my calves or the raking of my breath or the searing pain in my side as my body cramps up.

I don't even realize I've tripped until I tumble down a small embankment, rolling straight into a severed head.

If I had any breath left, I would have wasted it on the shrillest scream I could muster. It takes me longer than it should to recognize what the silhouette is. I blink twice and am suddenly confronted with the lost third of Enzo's triple-headed monster costume that I made out of papier-mâché only a few months prior.

I kick the head to the side and don't even bother to slow down as I burst through the tree line straight into a gathered crowd of friends who look both relieved and panicked to see me, and grown-ups who eye me suspiciously.

"Slow down, young man. This is a crime scene," says a mustached guy with glasses and a brown police officer's uniform.

"Where are you off to in such a hurry?" asks the other guy beside him, whose badge is on the waistband of his brown suit. He's got to be the "good cop" with his easy smile and fatherly worry. The first cop looks at him, annoyed. Guess he's the "bad cop."

"Crime scene?" I ask, looking immediately to my friends. Each one of them looks like they've just eaten some jellied onions.

"You know, people who answer questions with more questions usually become suspects," Bad Cop says.

"Suspects?" I ask.

"Another question," says Bad Cop, eyeing me even closer.

"Keith, you're scaring the poor kid," says Good Cop.

"I'm not scared," I say, a little offended.

"See? Not a question," says Good Cop to who I presume is Officer Keith. Then he turns to me. "I'm Officer Tapps. You can call me Dale."

He holds out his badge and extends his hand in a gesture that seems a little strange for me. I take it anyway, though. Seems rude not to. First, though, I slip the scrap of paper I found into my pocket. I thought I was being sly, but Officer Dale's eyes flick toward my hand before meeting my gaze again.

"Your friend here was just telling us about his story assignment for the newspaper," says Officer Dale smoothly before glancing over his shoulder. "Guess you've got a little more to report on now, son."

Enzo nods. He doesn't look happy about it, though. He's staring at something different than Officer Dale. He's eyeing the truck and full camera crew that's somehow managed to appear. There's a small cluster of crew members setting up canopies and camera tripods. Overseeing the whole scene is a tall, stalky guy hunched against the news van. He's wearing sunglasses, but his stare is intense enough to burn right through the lenses. Nothing is getting past this guy. In a weird way, he reminds me of my dad.

In a weird way. Not in a good way.

"Channel Four already scooped the story. Dad's gonna be so mad," Enzo says glumly.

Maritza nods, looking equally dejected. "It's going to be madcakes for sure tonight."

Madcakes? We all wait for an explanation.

Maritza shrugs. "Dad makes pancakes when work makes him angry. Madcakes. I don't know."

I wish *my* dad made madcakes when he was angry. Instead of, well . . . you know.

"Has anyone noticed lately how Channel Four seems to know about things before anyone else?" says Enzo, squinting at the crew in the distance.

"That's called quality reporting, young man," Officer Keith says, and his tone basically says that's the end of that.

Maritza isn't buying it. "Chet Biggs is *not* a quality reporter," she says.

"Chet Biggs," Enzo scoffs. "A made-up name if I've ever heard one. I think I'm gonna call myself Dan Bigmuscles from now on. Enzo Hastonsofallowancemoney."

"I heard the news director at Channel Four used to be the managing editor at the *Banner*," Trinity says, her eyes wide with conspiracy. "I can't imagine the people at the *Banner* were thrilled when the big boss decided to go work for the competition."

Officer Keith huffs. Officer Dale isn't looking at the Channel Four truck, though. He's looking at me.

"So, about that hurry you were in," he says, and this time he sounds a tinge less friendly. "Why were you in a rush?"

His question catches me off guard. "I . . . uh . . . found a head," I blurt out.

"You . . . found a head," repeats Officer Dale. Officer Keith puffs his chest beside him.

"A papier-mâché one," I explain. "Not a real one. It's, uh, a long story."

I almost think Officer Dale is going to ask for that whole long story until none other than Chet Biggs strides over to our little gathering at the other side of the construction site, his camera crew hustling to keep up.

"Detective Tapps," Chet Biggs says, clapping him on the shoulder. "Why don't you come on over and give us an exclusive. We'll make sure all of Raven Brooks sees that beautiful face of yours."

Officer Keith's chest deflates.

"Sorry, Chet, you know the drill. Open investigation and all that," says Officer Dale. Either Officer Dale is just friendly with everyone, or he already knows Chet Biggs. Officer Keith doesn't seem to be a fan of their friendship, judging by his scowl.

"Ah, come on, you know we're gonna find out one way or another. Might as well get your fifteen minutes of fame while you can," says Chet Biggs, and his focus shifts to Enzo with his notepad and official *Raven Brooks Banner* press pass lanyard, and Trinity with her parents' camera beside him.

"Hey, you're Esposito's kid, right?"

Enzo's grip on his pad tightens.

"Tell your pop if he ever wants a shot at the big time, we might be able to find him a junior reporter position," Chet says, a smile spreading slowly across his face.

I know I've gotta come in for the rescue.

"Mr. Biggs," I say, and the anchor turns to me. "I just wanna say I think it's really great that you're still willing to go on TV. Television screens are getting fancier every day, and it's inspiring that even though you're getting super old, you won't let a bit of wrinkles stop you."

His smile shrinks away.

I know I shouldn't continue but the look on Enzo's face—that shame, that naked embarrassment—I can't tell whose dad I'm thinking about anymore. Suddenly, all I want to do is destroy Chet Biggs.

"I mean, most people would have retired when they reached retiring age, but not *you*."

A crew member shouldering a video camera behind Chet stifles a laugh, and Chet reels around, silencing the cameraman with a stare.

"Chet, why don't I show you what I can," Officer Dale says, smoothly guiding the anchorman and his crew away, but not without one last stare from Chet McChetface.

I wave and smile.

Officer Keith leaves, too, with the most useless warning ever: "You kids stay out of trouble now."

Then it's just my friends, my sister, and me.

"Dude," Enzo says, his expression somewhere between awe and horror. "That was brutal."

"So, is someone going to fill me in on the big scandal here, or . . . ?" I say, remembering that I was just accused of stumbling into a crime scene.

"Someone vandalized the park," Trinity says.

"Again," says Maritza. "Last time was while you were in the hospital, just a day or two after the Unveiling Ceremony. It wasn't this bad, though. Just signs of a break-in. Some people thought that construction supplies were stolen, but no one could prove it."

I crane my neck to get a better view of whatever it is that's been taped off, but there are too many scenes to count.

"Basically, they spray-painted everything with a surface," says Enzo.

"It's like they have a thing against amusement parks," says Lucy. "I mean, who hates a Ferris wheel that much?"

Mya and I exchange a glance, but I don't think anyone noticed. They're all too busy trying to read the words scrawled in fuzzy, dripping paint, indeed sprayed across everything paint can stick to.

I don't have to look too hard, though.

"Cursed?" Maritza says, squinting across the construction site at a particularly marred concession stand.

"I count five 'Cursed's and three 'Omen's," says Trinity from behind her lens. She's busily snapping away at the damage.

"What's the point?" Lucy says. "They're just going to keep painting over it. It's not like the park isn't going to be finished eventually."

"What's this person so afraid of?" Enzo says.

"Who says it's just one person?" says Trinity.

Maritza shakes her head. "It's like they want other people to be afraid. Why else risk sneaking in here at night to do all this damage?"

Oh, I don't know, maybe to buy more time for construction? Maybe to distract from Mr. Gershowitz's disappearance?

I catch Mya looking at me again, and if I look half as

pale as she does right now, we don't stand a chance protecting any of our family's secrets for much longer.

"Okay, I'm just gonna say it," Maritza says. "Forest Protectors."

"Here we go again," says Enzo as he rolls his eyes, but is that his hand suddenly shaking over his notepad?

"Oh, because you're too intellectual to believe in it? Sorry, but whose costume head did Aaron just trip over on his way over to us?"

"Um, guys?" Lucy says from somewhere off in a cluster of trees at the edge of one of the taped-off areas. "You GUYS!" Lucy stomps from her place near the trees, and all heads meet her urgent stare.

Trinity is the first to see what she's holding.

"Maritza might not be too far off," Trinity whispers, taking the tangle of twigs and vines from Lucy's hand. Pierced through its middle is a long, shiny black feather.

Someone swallows their spit loud enough for me to hear. Maybe it was me.

"Do you think that's . . . evidence?" Enzo whispers. It's like we're all afraid of scaring the chunk of nest away.

"Maybe we should just leave it where we found it," Trinity says and sets it down carefully in the thicket of trees where Lucy spotted it.

None of us seems comfortable leaving it, but none of us seems comfortable being anywhere near it, either. We settle on leaving the scene, but not before Trinity can snap a couple of pictures of the vandalized areas that Channel Four isn't already swarming all over.

It's in that moment, when everyone else is busy examining the damage done to the site that was, until today, halfway constructed, that I think I see him.

He's so far away, and really, I can't be sure it's him at all. At this distance, I might be looking at a shadow cast by one of the zillions of trees that hasn't been cleared yet. I could be seeing the towering antenna from the Channel Four news truck. It could be a trick of the eye, the wrong slant of the sun. I don't think I'm seeing any of that, though.

I think I'm seeing my dad.

"Mya," I breathe, so quietly that she couldn't possibly hear me, so I nudge her with my elbow.

"Mya!" I hiss.

"Ow! What?"

"Shhh," I caution, but luckily, everyone else isn't paying attention.

I point in the direction I'd swear I just saw our dad. But by the time I lower my hand and stop pointing, he's gone.

If he was ever there in the first place.

"What?" Mya says, annoyed when she doesn't find anything.

"I thought I saw . . ."

"*What?*"

I shake my head. "Never mind. It was nothing."

Nothing. I tell myself over and over that it was absolutely, positively nothing. I say it so many times on the way back home that by the time we walk through the front door, I've convinced myself that my eyes were fooling me, that I was just in a heightened state of excitement. My nerves are getting the best of me.

"It was nothing."

I say it in my head the rest of the night through dinner, even though Mom is asking me questions about my day and Mya is asking me to pass the ketchup and Dad is too busy in his study to join us for dinner tonight.

I say it as I try to fall asleep, absolutely not seeing a mustache and argyle sweater peering around the corner of a tree trunk in the distance of the construction site, watching the fallout of his damage and relishing in the time he's bought himself.

I'm *definitely not* picturing him burying the evidence of whatever it is he knows about the disappearance of Mr. Gershowitz. Like a wallet.

When sleep still hasn't come by midnight and the rest of the house is wrapped in its nighttime quiet, I slip down from my bunk and switch on the desk lamp, illuminating the drawing I've been wrestling with for the last week. It's supposed to be the Square, the shopping area that basically the entire town hangs out at when it's not poking around the forest looking for bird people and graffiti. I'm struggling with the taco stand, though. It has this giant awning that casts a massive shadow over the sidewalk, but I keep getting the shading wrong.

Then I remember where I left my thick charcoal sticks.

The basement hasn't been mine ever since Mya revealed that it was hers. Or Dad's. But it's where my charcoals are.

I'm in front of the basement door before I remember that Dad's been locking it lately. Now that I know his study is down there, I suppose I understand why, even though it doesn't make it any less unsettling.

Tonight, though, it's unlocked, and I take that as a sign that it's okay to go down.

For tonight, the basement is mine.

Except it's not. Because the minute I reach the bottom of the stairs, there's my dad, sitting hunched on a metal folding chair I've never seen before, elbows in his lap, hands clasped in front of him, head down.

Dad doesn't even look up as I land clumsily in front of him, my former excitement at finishing my sketch suddenly a faraway memory.

Dad's face is obscured in shadow, but I can tell he isn't looking at me. It's like he doesn't even know I'm here, though that's impossible.

If he isn't talking, that means he must have seen me there today. That means *he* must have been there today. If he saw me, he knows I saw him, too.

"The world can be such a scary place," Dad says, his

voice so calm and even, I almost don't recognize it. His stillness should comfort me, but it has the opposite effect.

"I build fantasy lands that are supposed to make people forget that," he continues as he stares at the daylight paintings, "or at least put a barrier between them and the fear, just for a little while."

I try to focus on what Dad's saying instead of how he's saying it. In some ways, maybe I understand. What Dad does with his designs, that's sort of what I do with my drawings. I guess we're all trying to create an escape in some way.

"But what good is that if I can't protect my own family from the worst of it?" he says.

The worst of it. I can't tell if he's trying to confess something or obscure it. I can't tell if I'm supposed to understand any of this.

Whatever it is Dad's trying to tell me, it isn't something I'm going to understand tonight.

I forget entirely about the charcoals. Instead, I turn to leave without having said a single word.

Before I reach the top of the stairs, Dad's voice floats from the bottom to the top, reaching me just as I turn the knob.

"Don't watch TV tomorrow, Aaron," he says.

I don't sleep that entire night. Instead, I use a clay knife from my art kit and methodically carve a hole in the back of my desk, one that aligns perfectly with the missing

back of my desk drawer. After I've hollowed out the insu-
lation and tucked it into an old pillowcase, I place my stack
of sketches in the hole I've created, slide the drawer closed,
and wait for morning to come.

Maybe I don't have a safe space, but now my drawings
do. Maybe that'll be important someday. Maybe I'll be able
to look back and say I was able to stop the slow destruction
of my world in some way.

Chapter 5

As it turns out, avoiding TV was inconsequential. The story of the Golden Apple Amusement Park's vandalism problem and surrounding mysteries is everywhere.

It's blaring from the radio and the *Raven Brooks Banner*, thanks in part to Enzo's crack reporting and Trinity's pictures. So much for having someone on the inside. I can't really blame Enzo, though. He couldn't hide my secrets forever. Some secrets just don't keep.

It's on the lips of every gossip, from Mrs. Tillman at the natural grocer, to Mr. Anders at the auto shop, to loopy Mrs. Ryland in geography class.

It's in the eyes of every kid who doesn't know me but knows who I am, who stares at me as I slink down the halls, trying to move through the day unnoticed, even though that's easier said than done.

Thanks to Channel Four, the Peterson family legacy has not only been drudged up, but it's been made modern-day relevant. Apparently, the fine folks at Channel Four have been hard at work on a fascinating exposé on the legacy that Roger A. and Adelle R. Peterson left behind, from their mysterious and possibly dangerous experiments to their unceremonious booting from the weather station to their possible (probable?) involvement in the burning of the first Golden Apple factory. And what better reason to rehash every last salacious detail than to focus on the latest Peterson to enter the scene? What luck! There's a new kook to follow! Between the vandalism and accidents at the Golden Apple Amusement Park site to the disappearance of Ike Gershowitz—Mr. Ted Peterson's best friend—Channel Four

was able to gather enough material for a full thirty-minute segment to air on the morning news (and re-air tonight!).

Overnight, the Petersons have gone from town curiosity to a family of freaks.

Better still, if Channel Four was able to make all these connections to my family—whether they're real or not—speculation about what happened in Germany is sure to follow. How hard would it be to scour news stories from the year before we moved here? Surely, someone has a friend of a cousin's sister-in-law in Germany who could dig something up.

"It seems we have a celebrity in our class after all," Mrs. Ryland says, cocking an eyebrow at me in sixth period. Some of the class snickers, and I try to believe that Mrs. Ryland is only trying to lighten the situation, but I wish she didn't look like she was enjoying the drama so much.

So far today, I've gotten three spitballs to the back of my head, been tripped once in the hall, and was stared at more times than I can count. By the time I drag myself to Mr. Donaldson's eighth period, I wonder how hard it would be to widen that hole behind my desk and live out the rest of my days there.

"Give it two days," Enzo says as he slumps down in the desk beside me. "Some new scandal will break and you'll be old news."

"Right," I say hopelessly. "Because there's so much else

to talk about in Raven Brooks. Even talking about the weather brings up my family."

As if on cue, the storm that's been brewing outside suddenly sends cracking thunder loud enough to rattle the window at the far end of the room.

Enzo frowns. "I'm working on this story about raccoons," he says meekly. "About how they're destroying the sorghum crop out by the llama farm. Come next Tuesday, sayonara, Petersons, and hello, raccoons."

I look at Enzo.

I have to laugh. I have no choice. Through all of this, Enzo has not only stood by me, he's tried to save me from drowning in the murky pond that is my current life. I have to believe if he had any more self-respect, he'd run from me with the speed of a thousand stampeding horses.

"Whatcha laughing at, Doomsday?" Seth Jenkins says from my periphery. "Thinking about what your family's gonna burn down next?"

"New nickname," I say dryly, hoping Seth can't see just how close I am to snapping. "Clever. Been thinking of that all day?"

"Nah, just sort of came to me after I realized that you're, like, some kind of weird ghost kid."

Ruben Smith cackles beside Seth, scratching at his stiff hair as small flakes of dried gel sprinkle to the desk.

"Back off, Seth," Enzo warns, but Seth has an audience now. There's no way he's going to give that up.

"Seriously, how is it that the minute your creepy grandparents kick the bucket, it's all sunshine and rainbows around here," Seth sneers. "Then along come more Petersons and, bam! Storms and Forest Protectors and missing people, and what do they have to say about it? A big fat nothing."

The girl in the back who always chews her pencil stops chewing long enough to agree. "You have to admit, the coincidence is a little weird."

"He doesn't have to admit anything," Enzo growls. "He hasn't done anything wrong. *His family* hasn't done anything wrong."

I know that isn't true, and I'm grateful for Enzo's defense, but I'm having trouble feeling anything other than pure, white-hot rage at the moment.

"Tell that to Old Man Gershowitz," someone else says. I can barely see who, though. My vision is going fuzzy.

"Guys, c'mon, it's not his fault his family is probably into some weird sort of alien worship," someone else says.

"Who said anything about alien worship?"

"I mean, I think it's kinda obvious, don't you?"

My heart is racing so fast, I'm afraid it might fly out of my chest and splat onto the floor.

"I think it's obvious that nobody should be having dinner over at that house. Who knows what's in the hamburger?"

"Oh man, I had a hamburger at lunch."

Everything is shaking, from my legs to my fingertips. I

can feel my hand forming into a tight fist, but it doesn't feel like me doing it.

"Class, if we can't contain ourselves, everyone is going to be joining me for detention after school!"

"Probably safer in detention than out there with *him*."

"Uh-oh. What's wrong, Peterson?"

Seth is whispering just to me now. He's blurry, but his words are crystal clear.

"Look, man, don't worry," he breathes, dampening my ear. "Maybe the freak gene skips a generation. I'm sure you and your weird little sister will turn out just fine."

It's weird, but I don't even feel my fist hit Seth's jaw. Jaws are hard; it should make an impact. I'm completely numb, though. I hear the crack of his teeth as they snap together against the punch. I see a Seth-shaped blur crumple to the floor. I hear the initial shocked silence, followed by a chorus of voices shouting in unison.

"Fight! Fight! Fight!"

I see the class growing farther away as someone pulls me by my arm out of the room and into the hallway, down the corridor and into the administrative building we share with the elementary school.

Finally, as my senses return to my body in small, steady waves that move in unison with my slowing heartbeat, I pull Vice Principal Lee into focus. She's crouched at eye level with me. She looks not the least bit worried, and surprisingly not angry. She doesn't even look pitying. She looks at me like I'm a curiosity.

"Didn't think you had it in you," she says.

"I'm pretty sure everyone has a punch in them some-where," I say, surprisingly calm myself. Feeling has returned, but it's like every other life force has completely drained from me.

"You had to know a story like that was coming eventually," she says. She's talking to me like I'm a grown-up.

I'm not, though. I'm just a kid. Why can't anyone see that?

Vice Principal Lee stands, her knee joints popping as she does.

"Wait here for Principal Naveed."

The rest of the administrative office is buzzing with a low level of exhausted activity, and barely anyone bothers to look up at the student slumped in the chair at the far end of the hall.

Maybe I really am a creepy ghost kid.

If I am, though, I'm not alone.

A door from the opposite end of the long corridor swings open, and in walks my little sister, her head slumped, fists balled by her sides. Even with her head down, she looks taller somehow, like she's perched on a branch, peering at the world below her.

When she looks up, we lock eyes immediately, and I know I'm not the only one with a Seth in my eighth-period

85

class. And I guess I'm right. Everyone's got a punch in them somewhere.

* * *

Mom is less understanding than I thought she would be.

"Imagine my surprise!" she says breathlessly from the driver's seat, hitting pothole after pothole down the side road at the edge of the forest. Thanks to the storm that's now right on the edge of breaking, they've closed the main road back to our neighborhood.

"Imagine my utter astonishment! To get a call from not one but two principals from each of my kids' grades to tell me that each of my children has gotten into a fight at school. A *fight*!"

Obviously, it's harder for Mom to imagine than for Mya and me. We already knew how close we were to the edge. If I'm surprised about anything, it's that it didn't happen sooner.

"Imagine my outright shock to learn that my kids— my sweet, levelheaded, tender-hearted children—chose to resolve their conflicts with their fists rather than their words."

Seriously? Whose kids is she talking about? Mya and I are a lot of things, but levelheaded? That seems to be taking it a bit far. Mya and I swap looks.

"I saw that!" Mom yips from the front. "If you two think this is funny, then wait until you see what I have in store for you. You'll laugh your tushies off when I tell you how long you're grounded for!"

I hear Mya snort next to me, and I have to look away before her laugh spreads to me. It's super hard to take Mom seriously when she threatens us with words like "tushies."

"Oh yeah, you'll think it's a riot when I make you scoop the gutters out and stain the fence while all your friends are . . . doing whatever your friends do!"

Well, Mom, lately our friends stumble headfirst into possible crimes and conspiracies related to our family that lead us to resolve conflicts with our fists instead of our words, so . . .

"Trust me when I say you're going to find it hysterical when I take everything out of your rooms that brings you even an ounce of joy."

Uh-oh.

"Like those model car kits you found at the thrift shop, Mya? Say bye-bye!"

"But, Mom—!"

"And you can kiss your charcoals and sketchpad good-bye, Aaron."

"Mom, you can't—!"

"Oh, can't I? Can't I?"

I've never heard Mom this mad before. I've seen her sad, worried, bored, scared. I've even seen her peeved. But this is a whole new level, and I can barely recognize her as her eyes dart between us and the road, the rearview mirror only capturing half of her face. The angry half.

"You don't understand," I start to say, but clearly there is no worse thing to say than that.

"I don't understand? *I* don't understand?"

"Okay, okay, you understand," I hurry. "I take it back."

"I understand. You have no idea how much I understand!"

"No, no, you understand! You're the understanding-est. You're the queen of understanding. Your Royal Understanding-ness."

Mom takes a deep breath and blows it hard through her nostrils.

"We're sorry, Mom," Mya says, and I can tell she's on the verge of tears.

"Really, we mean it," I add.

Mom takes another nose-in, nose-out breath.

"I know you think I don't see what's happening," she says. "I've been married to your father for fifteen years. There's nobody in this world who knows that man better."

"Does that mean you know . . . about Grandma and Grandpa?" Mya asks timidly, and I'm probably horrible for being glad she was brave enough to ask first.

Mom gets quiet again, and I wonder if we've already pushed her too far.

Then she says, "A little."

Which sounds awfully close to "a lot."

Maybe it's because I'm tired of guessing. Maybe it's

because it feels like the car has somehow transported us to this place of post-punch understanding where all our secrets will be kept between the aluminum doors of our old car. Whatever it is, I finally ask.

"Do you think Dad could ever . . . like, do you think it's in him to do something . . . bad?"

Mom is quieter.

"Like, really bad?"

She's never been this quiet in her whole life. I can feel Mya staring at me while she waits to hear what Mom will say.

We don't get an answer, though, because suddenly, it's like we're on one of those whirligig rides where you spin yourself and the world spins around you, and your biggest hope is to not puke all over the person next to you. Tires are screaming and we're screaming and maybe this is how it all ends. Maybe this is the finale of the horror show that's been the past year and a half. Maybe the last thing I'll have done in my semipathetic life is to clutch my sister beside me in the car while my mom wrestles the steering wheel and tries to right whatever went wrong.

At least I got to punch Seth Jenkins before I died.

When the ride finally comes to a stop, the smell of burnt rubber and sweat fills the car.

And pee. I might have peed a little.

"We're okay. We're okay. We're okay," Mom keeps saying.

That's debatable, though. My seat belt digs into my collarbone as I pitch forward, and when I look beside me, Mya is angled the same way, tugging at the locked belt pressing against her.

Mom's in some kind of trance in the front seat, gripping the steering wheel with hunched shoulders and white knuckles. Mya's got a death grip on me that's going to cut off my circulation in a few seconds.

Mom's trance breaks, and she whips around, huge eyes scanning us up and down.

"You're okay? Yes? Tell me yes, please!"

Mya and I nod quickly. Anything to get her eyes to shrink back down to normal size. But I'm in one piece, and Mya's clearly got enough strength to squeeze the life out of me, so I'm guessing she's okay, too.

"It's all right, Mom," I say. I sound pretty frantic myself, though, so I'm not sure how much help I am.

We all stare at each other in silence for another minute until Mom finally unbuckles and steps out of the car to assess the damage. I hear a whisper followed by something less than a whisper, then Mom pounds her fist against the smoking hood of the car.

I get out, too, and Mom ushers me back into the car, even though there isn't a single car on the road to hit me. I manage to see the smoking hood, though, and the fact that we're jammed nose-first in a ditch.

Mya looks at me. I shake my head. Not good.

Mom slumps back into the driver's seat, tipping her head to the headrest and putting her hands over her eyes as she groans.

"What . . . happened?" Mya ventures, careful not to sound like she's blaming.

Mom gets super quiet again. I don't think she's even breathing.

"Mom?"

She shakes her head slowly, and I can't see her eyes in the rearview mirror anymore; she's sitting too far up. Now all I see is her neck, stretched and exposed. The artery jumps hard beside her throat. Her heart is still pounding. Maybe it's pounding harder now.

"I . . . I thought I saw something," she says quietly.

"What did you see?" Mya asks, but somehow, I already know.

Mom starts to laugh, and if she knew how hysterical she sounds, she'd probably stop right away.

"A bird," she says when she finally stops laughing.

Mya swallows. "A . . . *big* bird?"

Mom stops smiling. Then she nods, and that's all she has to say on that subject. Discussion over.

"Mom, was it a—" I start to say.

"It was nothing."

"But it had to have been a—" pleads Mya.

"*Nothing!*" she says, and Mya shuts her mouth tight.

Mom softens, looking guilty for snapping.

"We just had a scary thing happen. It's been a long, rotten afternoon, and now the car is stuck in a ditch," Mom says, switching fast to pragmatic Mom, and while the change is unnerving, at least this Mom is a little more familiar. "I need to walk to the service station."

I'm sorry, *what?*

"You can't go out—!" Mya and I say at the same time.

Mom holds up her palms as stop signs, cutting us both off.

"In case you've forgotten, I'm the parent in this car, and I've had more than my fill of arguments today," she says.

A jagged bolt of lightning lights the sky, and as the perfect punctuation on Mom's declaration, a loud crack of thunder shatters the air.

"If this storm gets worse, I want you kids here in a dry car and not out there in who-knows-what."

It's not the storm I'm afraid of, though, and judging by Mya's look of horror, I'm not alone.

Mom doesn't relent. "Stay put. Doors locked. Don't leave the car for anything. Got it?"

We nod.

And before we can utter the words "Forest" and "Protector," Mom is already a speck on the road ahead just before it winds around and she disappears toward the service station two miles ahead.

One good thing about coming from a family of chronic avoiders: Mya and I have quite the arsenal when it comes to distraction activities.

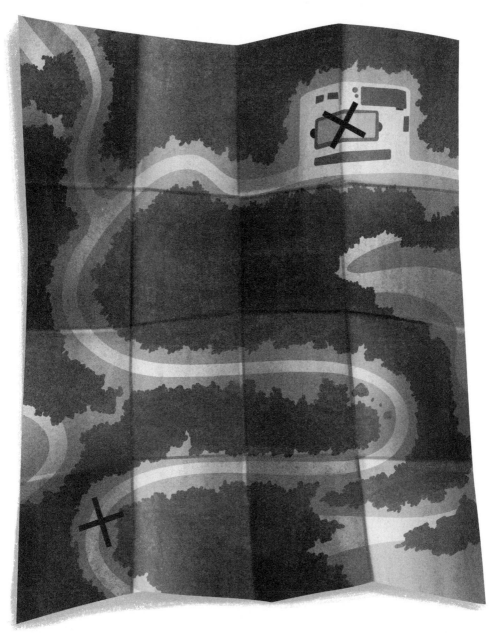

We play Would You Rather first.

"Would you rather . . . eat a caterpillar or listen to Aunt June sing?"

Mya chooses the caterpillar.

Next, we play our own improved version of rock, paper, scissors.

"Rabid dog beats rack of lamb!"

"Nope, this is *zombie* lamb. Dog bites zombie lamb, zombie lamb bites back. I win."

I beat Mya five times before we switch games.

We're three rounds into I Smell: Bodily Gases Edition before we notice the time.

"She's been gone for forty minutes," Mya says, staring down the road like she can wish Mom into existence.

"The service station is probably just busy," I say, purposely not flinching at the massive raindrops that have been pounding the roof of the car for the last twenty-seven minutes, not that I've been counting.

"She'll be back any minute," Mya agrees, even though obviously we both disagree.

But then Mya's eyes shoot skyward. Something is tapping the roof of the car.

"Just an animal, maybe," I breathe, holding perfectly still.

"Out in a storm?" Mya says, and this is the worst time in the world for her to make sense.

The tapping stops, and for a second, I venture a deep breath.

That is, until the tap turns into a long, horrifying scratch.

The scratch reaches the middle of the roof, directly over our heads, and I see Mya's hand move to the door handle. I nod, or at least I think I do, but we both understand.

The scratch continues forward, methodically, until it reaches the top of the cracked windshield.

We don't wait to see. We need to get out of the car *now*. Mya spins down the handle, and we run out into the rain.

We bolt for the tree line across the empty road, sprinting between sheets of downpour, lighted by the occasional streak of lightning.

"Here! Over here!" I yell over the howling wind, grasping Mya's hand and pulling her toward a knot of trees entangled with vines.

I slip and slide on fallen leaves and mud, and I can hear Mya gasping and gulping through the relentless rain.

"C'mon!" she yells, pulling ahead of me and yanking at my arm as I scramble back to my feet and follow her lead. It's like every part of the forest is trying to swallow us up or spit us out, I can't tell. All I know is no part of it wants to protect us.

"Did it follow us?" Mya hollers over her shoulder, but I have no idea. I try to look backward, but I can only manage a split second before I have to turn around and navigate the thick maze of trees.

I stumble right over Mya, and we both pull back to our feet and sprint in unison, holding tight to whatever we can find on the other—a shirt sleeve, a wrist, a finger.

When we finally break through an overgrown knot

of brush, we find ourselves suddenly in a small clearing where only a patch of grass has managed to grow.

I back against Mya, and she backs against me, and we squint through the fat drops and circling wind while we slowly rotate, searching between every opening in the thatched woods around us. We're not in the trees anymore, but we're far from safe.

"Mya," I breathe, not sure my voice can even reach her over the storm. "Can you see it?"

I feel Mya's head shake against mine.

"Do you think it's gone?" she whispers back.

I shake my head.

Through the streaks of rain and flickers of lightning, I watch as a tree branch bows and bends to the side, making way for something to come through.

"Mya?"

I can feel her trembling against my back, and she reaches for my hand and squeezes it tight.

"Something's coming!" she says, staring in her own direction. I grasp her other hand as we brace ourselves for what will emerge from the woods.

I don't see anything, though. I can't. I'm temporarily blinded by a light bright enough to illuminate the entire forest.

"Hold it right there!" says a voice that sounds familiar, but I can barely breathe, let alone identify whatever is holding that ridiculously bright light.

"What do we have here?"

* * *

Officer Keith could not be more pleased with himself. He looks like a wilderness scout about to earn his crime-fighting badge. His yellow rain slicker is streaming puddles onto the hardwood in the foyer.

"Lucky we found 'em when we did," he says, clearly unhappy with the praise he's not getting. "They're saying this storm's gonna be a record breaker."

Mom and Dad aren't concerned about the storm, though. Mom won't stop holding on to Mya and me. She has us wrapped up in blankets like burritos on the couch.

Dad is standing in the foyer with pasty Officer Keith and Detective Dale, whose easy company is rubbing Dad the wrong way. I don't think he buys the whole good cop routine. He sees something in Detective Dale he doesn't like. I can tell by how flat his eyebrows are.

"What about 'stay in the car' was unclear?" Mom says through gritted teeth.

"Aw, now, Mrs. Peterson, it's clear the kids got scared. Try not to go too hard on them," Detective Dale says smoothly.

Dad's eyebrows form a horizontal line.

"Well, I'm glad we were able to get you all home safely," Detective Dale says, clearing his throat once he determines he isn't going to get much thanks for scaring the pants off of us and making my mom feel like America's Most Wanted for abandoning her kids in a storm.

There's something else, though, a tension I can't locate. Dad looks like he's ready to bite one of their faces off. I just can't tell which one. I'd settle for either, to be honest.

"Have yourselves a good night," Officer Keith says, not bothering to mop up his puddles before stepping back outside.

Sergeant Dale is about to follow him out when he turns and leans toward my dad, a smile on his face that feels far from easy.

"And thanks again for agreeing to come in tomorrow, Ted. We just have a few unanswered questions about that vandalism. I'm sure you'll be able to clear it up in no time. We all want what's best for the park's construction, right?"

If Dad's eyebrows had the power to vaporize a person, this would be the time to test it out. Instead, Mom chimes in from the couch, loud enough to make my ears ring.

"Oh, Detective, congratulations on your promotion! You must be so proud. By the way, how is the search coming for Ike Gershowitz? You know we all want what's best for our friend, right?"

It's a blink-and-you'd-miss-it slip, but suddenly, Detective Dale's affable facade slides away, and behind it lies a look so venomous, I'm compelled to sit up tall enough to shield my mom from his stare.

When my dad closes the door, he turns to us, and I brace for impact.

Instead, he does something strange.

He says, "I'm sorry."

Then he walks down the back hallway, and I hear the basement door open gently and close. The confusion Dad leaves in his wake is almost more than I can take after the day I've had.

Mya is the one to talk first.

"I want to go to bed."

Mom doesn't argue.

We both shuffle into our respective bedrooms. After an hour of staring at the ceiling in my room and waiting for my body to finally stop trembling, I hear my door creak open, and Mya's tiny frame settles into the bottom bunk.

"It all comes back to the Forest Protectors," she says softly, starting a conversation in the middle because she knows I've been thinking about it for an hour, too.

"I know," I say.

"The thing you chased through the tunnel after finding Mr. Gershowitz's wallet, the articles Enzo found about the weather and the nests being connected somehow, Grandma and Grandpa's research? It all comes back to the Forest Protectors. And then tonight . . ."

"I know," I repeat.

"Okay, so if you know so much, what do we do about it?" Mya asks, and I can't tell if she's annoyed or desperate.

"We have to go back to the weather station."

"No way."

And now I *can* tell what she is: terrified.

"Mya, listen to me. The answers are in Grandma and Grandpa's office—"

"In the weather station. In the middle of the forest," she says. "I'm not going back there."

"Listen to me," I say, maybe a little too loudly.

"Aaron, no way—"

"Just listen!"

Mya gets quiet, and I climb down from my bunk and sift through my dirty clothes hamper until I find the jeans I was wearing when the vandalism was discovered.

I pull the folded sheets of worn paper from my pocket and spread them on the floor beside the lower bunk where Mya is lying on her side.

She leans close to the floor, squinting through the dark at the writing on the pages.

"These are from their notebook," she says, making the connection to the handwriting and the tiny paper.

"I found it by the tree where the nest was," I say. "I was going to show you before the whole graffiti thing."

Mya moves her hands over the words on the page like she's trying to decipher their meaning through touch. Then she gets to the list of names.

I wait until she looks back up at me.

"Whatever Grandma and Grandpa were working on, it has something to do with the strange weather, and the weather has to do with the Forest Protectors, and right now, everyone's happy to put our family right in the middle of that whole mess."

I point to the short list of names on the last page of our grandparents' notes.

"This is the first bit of proof I've found that indicates maybe someone else knows more than we do. Maybe someone else made this mess."

I can already see Mya's fear crumbling under new bravery. She's propped on her elbow now.

"There are answers in that weather station," I say. "Grandma and Grandpa knew something, but they never got to finish their work."

Mya sighs away the last of her resolve. "So, we need to help them finish it."

I tuck the folded papers into my middle desk drawer and climb back to my bunk, letting the now steady wind and rain lull me into a restless sleep. My last thoughts are about how to creep out from under the watchful eye of a newly protective Mom in order to get to the weather station without detection. One way or another, Mya and I will go. We have to. For the first time since I woke up in that hospital bed with a skull-rattling headache, I hope that I'll be able to take control of the tornado that is my life.

Except that sometime during the night, a different, literal tornado touches down in Raven Brooks and ruins everything.

Chapter 6

RAVEN 🌐 BROOKS 🌐 BANNER

MICRO-BURST WREAKS HAVOC ON RAVEN BROOKS:
Yet More Delays In Store for Golden Apple Amusement Park

*R*aven Brooks experienced some of its fiercest lightning on record early Wednesday night, Meteorologists have dubbed the storm a "microburst," due to its sudden and erratic behavior and potential for destruction.

Those who witnessed the storm for themselves, however, are naming it something else.

"A tornado!" said Marvin Buxbaum, 41, of Potters Court. "I spent half my life in Tornado Alley from Kansas and Oklahoma. I know a twister when I see one."

Nelly Grisham, 29, of Silver Lakes agreed. Pointing to the shattered window of her upstairs bedroom and two downed trees in her yard, she said, "The wind was just swirling. You could barely hear over the ruckus."

Clayton Park, 55, assessed the damage at his Korean BBQ located in the Square, an area hit particularly hard by the fierce storm. He told the Raven Brooks Banner *that he feels lucky to have survived unscathed. "Everyone said I was going overboard with cardboard in my windows, but it just seems like these storms are getting worse and worse. And if anyone in the neighborhood needs a safe place to eat, bad weather or no, Park's BBQ is the place to be!"*

According to Dr. Lucia Rivera of the Modern Weather Institute, "The phenomena in Raven Brooks are not only growing more frequent, their behavior is less predictable. The fact that it seems to be isolated to this particular town makes the whole thing even more baffling, and frankly concerning."

The bad weather has prompted locals to wonder about the future of Golden Apple Amusement Park, slated to open this summer. Mayor Marvin Tavish remains unconcerned.

"Things are humming along nicely. Beautifully, in fact!" Mayor Tavish said in an exclusive interview with the Banner. *"By this summer, Raven Brooks will be known internationally for two things: delicious candy and the best family recreational park this side of the Mississippi."*

The Golden Apple Amusement Park has been plagued by several delays, twice due to vandalism and once after a crane operator was injured by falling pipework. Furthering the amusement park's troubles has been the yet unexplained disappearance of a security guard tasked with patrolling the construction site. In recent weeks, the park's very own designer—Theodore Peterson—has come under increased scrutiny, leading some to believe the park's troubles are connected to more than just the weather.

"Think about it," said Joanie Jenkins, 49, who identified herself as a local mother. *"Here comes this family out of nowhere, and suddenly the storms are back and worse than ever. Now you tell me if that's just coincidence."*

"The people of Raven Brooks have nothing to worry about," said Mayor Tavish. *"Construction is proceeding as scheduled, and our rides will be bigger and better than any you've ever seen. Come rain or shine, the citizens of our happy little town will be screaming their heads off this summer."*

Enzo takes a deep sigh, folds the newspaper in half, and sets it on the floor.

"Well, at least you aren't the only thing people are talking about anymore," he says to me.

I think I'd prefer raccoons.

"No," I say, doing nothing to hide my sarcasm. "We're just at the center of all the bad stuff."

"I dunno," says Maritza from across the room, mashing her thumb into the controller as she applies a triple kick to my sister's man-bear. "If you ask me, the Forest Protectors are the stars of the show."

"Argh, quit that!" Mya says. "My stubby bear legs can't kick you back."

"Just bite my face," says Maritza.

"There *were* those random kids who say they found a nest," Trinity says in defense of Maritza. "Practically right on top of where you two ran into the forest."

"Where we *got chased* into the forest," Mya corrects, and I stifle a chill at the memory of that hideous scratching on the roof of the car.

"Which is exactly why they're not letting anyone in the forest anymore. Official construction business only," pouts Enzo. "No reporters allowed. Junior or otherwise."

"It's not like the nest would still be there anyway," I say. "They never are." I feel bad for him. His gig as a junior reporter for the *Banner* was everything to him. He scheduled his entire year around it.

"Bet Channel Four will find a way into the woods," he grumbles.

"Nah, they're too busy reporting on the 'storm of the century,'" Trinity says, trying on her Chet Biggs voice.

"They act like no one's ever seen a tornado," Maritza says, using her scorpion tail to paralyze the man-bear.

"Microburst," Trinity corrects.

"I mean, it did take down the power grid for a good three days," says Enzo, shuddering. "I had to read a book . . . by candlelight."

"Don't act like you don't like to read," says Maritza, restarting the game.

"I do, but not by candlelight," he says.

"I don't think people are weirded out by the tornado," I say, trying to move away from what's clearly a very traumatic memory for Enzo. "I think it's that people think it's getting worse."

"It *is* getting worse," Trinity says. "You weren't here before, but trust me, it's never been this bad."

My stomach twists, and it must show on my face because she adds, "Not because of you guys. That's ridiculous."

Obviously. Ridiculous.

"I could have been camping with Lucy and her family," Maritza says, reflecting on her own rotten luck.

Mya drops the controller and gives up, turning to join the conversation instead of losing to Maritza again.

"Can you die of boredom? Like, can you literally die? Because I feel like I'm going to drop dead if I have to play one more video game."

"Jeez, I'll let you win next time, okay?" Maritza says, and at least I'm not the only one feeling a little stir-crazy.

"It's not you," Mya says. "It's all these new rules. 'No going into the forest!' 'No staying out past eight!' 'No talking to human-sized birds!'"

"You made that last one up," says Trinity.

"Well, it's implied," Mya says.

"Why would you *want* to talk to one?" says Enzo.

"Oh, I don't know. To ask them what the heck they are? What's up with their nests? Do they really drink the blood of children?"

"Wow, I hadn't heard that one," I say, trying to banish the image of that particular horror.

"Maybe you should talk to that group of kids from the news who say they saw one when they snuck out past curfew the other night," I say.

"See, that's what I'm talking about!" Mya says, still grumpy, and she's going to make all of us suffer for it. "All this bonkers stuff is happening, and all our parents or the police or even the news people—" She turns to Enzo. "No offense."

"None taken."

"—all anyone in charge can tell us is that we're imagining things, there isn't anything weird going on, but keep out of the woods and don't go out after dark."

"Okay, so we make them tell us what's going on," I say, drawing skepticism from all sides of the room.

"Because we're so trustworthy?" asks Enzo.

"Because we're so smart," I say, tapping my temple and eliciting a snort from Maritza.

"What?" If I was trying not to sound defensive, I clearly failed.

"Nothing, nothing!" says Maritza, absolutely not hiding her smirk.

"Look," I say, grabbing a notebook from the table where Enzo writes.

At the top, I write WEIRDNESS, then start my list:

I leave out the part about the wallet I haven't seen since waking up in the hospital. That one's just for Mya and me, at least for now.

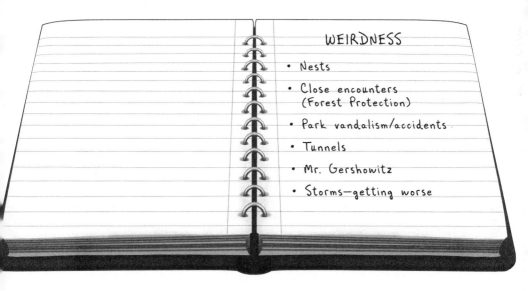

WEIRDNESS

- Nests
- Close encounters (Forest Protection)
- Park vandalism/accidents
- Tunnels
- Mr. Gershowitz
- Storms—getting worse

I tap my pencil on each item as I read it aloud.

"These are things we know are happening. What we don't know is why," I say.

"And the papers," Mya says, and my entire body flushes hot as I remind myself that not all family secrets have to be kept, at least not from my friends, who are probably just about the only people in the universe trying to help (or who believe me). If my grandparents' notes can help us find the connection between all the seemingly random oddities in Raven Brooks, then I have no choice but to share the pages from their notebook I found by the tree.

So, I do it. I spill everything.

"Hang on, who else was on that list?" Enzo says afterward. He's getting some of his journalism mojo back.

"I just recognized Mayor Tavish. There were other names, but I can't remember," I say.

"And that might not have even been the whole list," Mya adds. "The page was ripped."

"And who knows what that list even meant?" Trinity says. "It could be anything!"

Mya is scanning our own list while we debate my grandparents' notes. She sits up suddenly.

"Forest Protectors," she says.

"Yessss!" Maritza says, enthused for the first time this afternoon. "*Now* things are getting interesting!"

I examine the list. "Mya's right. In the tunnels, I was

chasing one of those things. And the storms always come right after there's a huge swarm of crows."

"Murder," Enzo corrects, evoking Mrs. Ryland.

"Right. Thanks for that," I say drolly.

"But the park vandalism? Mr. Gershowitz?" Trinity says. "I dunno."

"Mr. Gershowitz's wallet," I say. "I found it right before I started following the Forest Protector out of the tunnel. And Lucy found that piece of a nest near the park that day, remember?"

"Your grandparents must have seen the connection, too," says Trinity.

"Yeah, and someone didn't want anyone else seeing it," I say, remembering the frayed edges of those pages torn from their notebook.

"We need to get back to their weather station," Enzo says.

"Great," says Maritza, her enthusiasm waning. "So, we're back to where we started. We're banned from the forest, remember? Official Golden Apple Amusement Park construction only."

Mya and I exchange a look. I guess this is it. I nod, giving her the okay.

"What if there was another way into the tunnels?" says Mya.

Chapter 7

"This is a fantastically horrible idea," Enzo says. "Like, in the history of horrible ideas, this one ranks right under taking a ride on the *Hindenburg*."

"That actually wasn't the worst zeppelin tragedy in history. The USS *Akron* crashed into the sea four years earlier and killed almost twice as many people."

We all turn to look at Mya.

"That's a weird, random fact to have stored away in your brain," Enzo says.

"She's got a lot of those," I say.

Then I refocus my attention on the tunnel. We're supposed to be having a sleepover, which was hard enough to convince my mom to let us do. If she were to catch us down here—if *Dad* were to catch us down here—I'm not sure I'd ever see the outside of this basement again.

"Can we just get on with this?" I say nervously.

"Do we even know what it is we're getting on with?" asks Maritza.

"Guys, am I the only one wondering why there's apparently a whole network of tunnels that runs underneath the entire town?" Trinity chimes in. "Or why one of the passages leads straight to this house?"

Mya and I share a look through the dark of our dad's basement office. No, she's not the only one wondering. Not by a long shot.

I take the deepest breath of my life. I guess there's no dancing around it now.

"I don't know why the tunnels are here," I say slowly.

I look one last time at Mya. If she gives me any sign I should stop here, I'll shut my mouth forever.

But she doesn't.

"We think that our grandparents knew why, though," I say. "And that maybe they . . . used them."

No one says a word. Maybe they already guessed. Maybe they were just waiting for me to finally admit it.

"They might not have been entirely innocent," I say.

I can almost smell the fumes of the first Golden Apple factory burning. I can practically see my grandparents fleeing, ducking into the weather station and slipping through the hidden door to the tunnels, running all the way back to their own basement to bask in their revenge on the Tavish family.

I'm so lost in my family's dark past, I don't feel Enzo's hand on my shoulder at first.

"We won't tell," he says.

I blink myself back to the dark basement to see Maritza and Trinity each holding tight to my sister's hands.

"If we find anything," Trinity says, and Maritza nods, "we won't say a word. We'll keep your secret."

I had no idea secrets were so heavy. Carrying them around becomes a habit, I guess, and pretty soon, you just assume that weight is a part of you. Once in a while, though, you get to put the weight down. Or someone takes one end of it while you take the other.

My shoulders lift for the first time in months.

"Well, we're not going to find anything unless we, you know . . . go in," Maritza says, pulling us all back to the dark, endless tunnel before us. An unwelcome memory slides through my brain—a tapping, or maybe a dragging, echoing down the passage in its darkest part. The sound of talons.

"We've come this far," says Trinity. "I vote we go in."

"So do I," says Maritza.

Mya and I nod in unison. "We're in."

All eyes shift to Enzo. "Not exactly leaving me much choice, are you?" he grumbles.

"C'mon," I say, nudging Enzo. "Think about how much material you could gather for the *Banner*! I can guarantee you Chip Biggbutts hasn't stepped foot in one of these tunnels before."

"Yeah, that's probably why he's still alive, annoying all of us every weeknight."

I click on the flashlight I snuck from the kitchen drawer before we came down. "You could always stay here and stand guard," I say.

"And face your dad when he catches us? No, thanks," Enzo says, grabbing the flashlight from me. "I'll take my chances with the Forest Protectors."

As Enzo leads the way, I walk alongside him, doing my best to remember which passage leads where, but I've never entered the tunnels from this point. I'm trying to concentrate, but the conversation behind me is hard to block out.

"What if they're some sort of human-bird hybrid your grandparents invented?" Maritza posits.

"They were meteorologists, not Dr. and Dr. Frankenstein," Mya says.

"All that weather stuff could have been a cover, though," Maritza persists. "I mean, who's going to ask follow-up questions about weather patterns?" She starts to snore as she walks.

"Mrs. Ryland," Trinity snorts.

"What if it's all one big joke?" Trinity says. "Like, a bunch of kids just taking an urban legend and running with it to scare people?"

Mya wastes no time disputing that theory. "It's no joke. Whatever chased us was real," she says, and suddenly, I'm in the forest with her, running through the rain and backing against my sister as we wait to be pecked to death.

Which is why it's even weirder that *I* was the one chasing one of *them* that day I first discovered the tunnels and Mr. Gershowitz's wallet.

"So," Enzo says beside me as I pluck my way through

the narrow, dank passages and try not to trip in the dark. "How come you never told me about *Fernweh Welt*?"

* * *

Either I just stepped into a particularly sludgy spot in the tunnels, or that's my entire soul draining out of my body and onto the ground.

I stop hard enough for Mya, Maritza, and Trinity to crash into us.

"What? What do you see?" Trinity breathes, poking her head between Enzo's and my shoulders.

"N-nothing," I stumble. "I just thought . . . it's nothing."

"If you could keep the dramatics to a minimum, that would be fantastic," Maritza scolds. "I'm already a little on edge here."

"Sorry," I whisper, then I keep walking because if I do what I really want to do, it would mean turning on my heel and stampeding back to my house, locking myself in my room, and never coming out.

"Didn't know it was such a touchy subject," Enzo quips, but I can tell by the way he says it that he had to know it was something.

"It was just an amusement park," I say, staying as oblique as I can. "My dad's designed tons of those."

It's taking everything I have to keep my cool. I've never wanted Mya's interruption more than I do now, but she's still exchanging Forest Protector theories behind me.

"Look, if you don't want to talk about it . . ." Enzo says, and I have never wanted to talk about anything less, but now it's all I can think about.

"It's just I've had a lot of time on my hands since we haven't been allowed into the forest," he continues, failing miserably at sounding casual. He's worse at faking it than I am.

"Anyway, after Channel Four ran that smear piece on your family—"

"It wasn't just about my family," I correct, but it *was* about my family, and we both know it.

"Anyway, it got me thinking about your dad's other parks because, I mean, maybe if people knew how . . . er, *not* scary . . . he is . . ."

It might be dark in here, but I can still see Enzo struggling.

He gives up. "Okay, well, if people knew how *not homicidal* he is . . ."

I guess that's better?

"Whatever, I found out there was an accident at the last park," Enzo blurts.

I guess he's a believer in that whole ripping-off-the-Band-Aid approach.

Things go quiet behind us, and it appears the Forest Protector discussion has ceased in favor of something more interesting.

"Wait, what last park?" Trinity pipes up.

"*Fernweh Welt* . . . what language is that?"

"What sort of accident?"

"Whoa, did someone *die*?"

"Stop!"

Mya's voice pings from damp wall to damp wall, ringing over and over her one-word plea, echoing through all of our ears until it fades to little more than a whisper. We wait for every last echo to cease.

"Yes, it was in Germany," Mya says all in one breath. "Yes, someone died. No, we don't know anything else. It was horrible and can we please not talk about it anymore because it's bad enough I have to dream about it!"

Maritza doesn't even wait a beat before throwing her arms around my sister, and once again, Maritza is my absolute favorite person ever. That is, until Trinity slings her long arm over my shoulders, and Enzo bows his head in some sort of silent apology.

"We don't have to talk about it," Trinity says quietly. "Any of it."

Afterward, all I can concentrate on is just how much Enzo managed to learn about our time in Germany and our sudden departure from it.

What if he eventually decides that he knows too much, and being my friend simply isn't worth bearing the weight of so many secrets? Could I really blame him?

"Ouch! What the—!"

Maritza's sudden cry is enough to bring me out of my head and back to the tunnels. This time I shine the light behind me and onto Maritza's crouched figure. She's bent at her waist, clutching her ankle.

"It felt like something bit me!" she says, rubbing her skin.

"Please don't say that," Mya cringes, searching the damp tunnel floor behind her.

Then Maritza reaches behind her foot and pulls something out of the thin line of fetid water.

A long, shiny black feather.

"Oh, I really wish I hadn't seen that," Enzo says.

"Okay, I'm officially creeped out," Trinity says. "Aaron, please tell me we're getting close because I think I've had about enough of creeping through smelly tunnels."

In quite possibly the worst case in history of bad timing, I have a sudden realization.

I don't exactly know which tunnel leads to the weather station.

"It's . . . uh, I mean, I'm pretty sure it's just right around the . . . or at least close to the, um . . ."

"You have no idea where you're going," Trinity says, the whites of her eyes glowing bright in the tunnel.

"He knows," Mya says, and I'm grateful for her defense, but I'm about to hyperventilate because if I'm being totally honest, I barely remember my time in the tunnel. It's not like I was in the most relaxed state of mind.

"Let's not panic," Enzo says, an unlikely voice of reason. He grabs the flashlight from my hand. "I mean, how many tunnels could there really—"

He shines the beam just a few feet from where I'd been aiming it, and openings to five different tunnel passages yawn before us.

"Oh, come *on!*" Enzo says, shoving the flashlight back into my hands.

"We can always turn around," Mya says to a chorus of objection.

"And do this all over again?"

"When are we going to get another chance?"

"There's no way!"

"Does anyone actually know the way back?"

The last question might not have been so scary if it hadn't come from my own mouth.

"Yep. Definitely going to be sick," Trinity says, clutching her stomach.

I swing around, shining the light as far as I can down each tunnel, looking for something—*anything*—familiar.

That's when the beam lights on something reflective.

I run toward it, but I don't even need to get close to know what it is I'm looking at—a triangular shard of glass. Kind of like the glass from a broken lantern.

Soggy footsteps pad behind me to catch up.

"I've been here," I breathe.

"Are you sure?" Trinity responds.

I nod. There's no question. This is where I found Mr. Gershowitz's wallet.

"We have to be close."

I shine the light down the tunnel and pick up my pace. It isn't long before we reach another fork in the tunnel, and we're staring at two identical passages.

"I don't remember this," I say, digging around in my memory for some recollection of choosing a passage. I can't remember much more than panic, though, and of course the acute fear that spread through me at the sight of that smeared blood on Mr. Gershowitz's wallet.

"Think, Aaron!" Maritza urges.

"I'm trying!"

But it's no use. My memory is as dark as these tunnels.

So, I do what any rational person would do in this situation. I pretend.

"This way!"

When we hit a dead end, I know the jig is up. So much for faking it.

"Okay, Marco Polo, time for someone else to take the lead," Trinity says, yanking the flashlight from my hand.

"Wait a minute," Mya says, running her fingers along the walls.

"I wouldn't do that," Maritza says, wrinkling her nose. "It's like Hotel Bacteria down here."

"She's looking for something," Trinity says, catching on first.

"A door," I say.

Of course. The passage in the weather station was covered up. So was the one in the basement.

Soon, we're all running our hands along the wall, pressing anything that feels like it might give.

"Please don't let me touch a spider. Please don't let me

touch a spider," I hear Enzo whispering over and over to himself in one corner.

Great. Now I'm worried about smooshing a spider with my bare hands.

"Hang on. What's—"

Mya doesn't even get to finish. Instead, I hear a weird grinding sound, and a thud, followed by a grunt and the smell of old paper and mildew.

"I'm okay," Mya says, but she sounds strangely far away.

When I step through the opening she uncovered, I understand why.

The drop is at least five feet, and I narrowly miss landing right on top of my sister. We both roll out of the way in time to miss being crushed by Enzo's giant feet. At least he lands better than I did. My tailbone might never be the same.

Same goes for the flashlight. I might have landed bottom first, but my landing popped the cover from the battery compartment, sending both batteries scattering to the darkest corners of whatever it is we've fallen into.

"Maybe one of us should stay outside to—" I start to say, but I'm too late. Maritza and Trinity land with two hard thunks.

"I . . . don't think this is the weather station," Mya says, feeling her way around the dim room. It's nearly impossible to see, with only a meager light shining from the night sky above. The fact that we can see the sky at all is pretty remarkable, though.

"Are those windows?" Maritza asks, tilting her head as far back as it will go.

"I think this might be an observatory of some kind," Trinity says, switching her gaze skyward and back to the room, which, if I stare really, really hard, looks almost hexagon-shaped. No, octagon. There are eight walls, at least that I can count. Every corner is darker than the last.

I try making my way toward wherever I'm pretty sure I saw a battery roll when my toe slips into a deep groove carved into the floor.

"Aaron," Mya whispers from across the room. I'm not sure why we're all whispering, but this seems like the kind of place where you'd whisper. Kind of like a combination between a library and a laboratory.

I abandon my search for the battery and make my way toward her. She's holding a notebook full of handwriting I could recognize in my sleep by now.

"Grandma and Grandpa's notes," I say.

Mya nods. Like the folded bundle of pages I found by the tree, these papers are covered in the same indecipherable notations and equations that meant something to my grandparents but absolutely nothing to us.

But the notebook is *here*, in this room. Which means maybe Grandma and Grandpa were, too.

"Um, guys?" Enzo says, and I don't like the way his voice is shaking.

When I turn, he's pinching a long, dark cloak between

his fingers. The hood of the cloak comes to a sharp point just past the shoulders.

"Whoever owns this might be back for it," Enzo agrees, dropping the cloak.

I'm just starting to figure out how we can hoist each other through the opening above when the floor begins to shake.

"Please tell me you feel that, too," Mya utters.

"I feel it."

"Is that . . . thunder?" Maritza says, bracing herself against a wall as the shaking gets stronger.

"That doesn't sound like thunder," Trinity says. "That sounds like a freight train!"

All at once, the sound is upon us, and the floor beneath feels like it's sliding and jumping. Complete darkness swallows the night sky, and the din is so loud, I pull myself into a tight ball and cover my ears.

The sound of millions of crows screeching through the sky fills the eight-walled room, the scant spaces between their beating wings revealing a sky now swirling an unearthly green.

I grab for Mya, but she tumbles away from me, losing her footing on the rippling floor.

Trinity rolls toward me, and I grasp her hand and lead us toward a wall, but small chunks of stone begin falling from it, dropping dangerously close to our heads. We duck and cover, and soon, all I can feel is a shower of small rocks, and all I can hear are the cries of countless birds.

Then I hear the door to the passage above slam shut.

Chapter 8

The room is going to split apart. I'm sure of it.

I venture a look at the corner behind me and find Mya and Maritza clinging to each other, doing their best to dodge falling stone. At the other side of the room, Enzo hasn't managed to regain his footing. A piece of the wall is rattling loose above him.

"Enzo!"

I break from Trinity's grip and dive for Enzo, sliding us both to the corner closest to the rumpled cloak right before the chunk of wall falls.

From this angle, I see the glowing floor for the first time. It looks almost radioactive, the vibrant light fading from purple to green and back to purple all along the small grooves etched into the floor that crisscross the room.

"What the . . . ?"

The noise from the birds reaches a new decibel, and we're all forced to cover our ears once again.

Then, just as soon as the chaos began, it stops, leaving in its wake a silence so thick, it stifles the air.

I think it's my imagination until I see the others slowly rise to their feet, holding their arms out to examine the hairs standing on end. Enzo's hair looks like it's grown to twice its size.

I reach for a newly formed crack in the stone wall and snatch my hand away at the bright spark that stings me.

As though it occurs to us all in the same moment, five pairs of eyes look to the tunnel opening five feet above, its door shut tight.

"Don't panic. Nobody panic!" Enzo says a little too loudly.

"Pretty sure you're the only one panicking," Maritza says.

"I might not be too close behind," Trinity admits, still fixated on her gooseflesh.

"You saw the lights, right?" Mya says frantically. "I wasn't the only one who saw that, right?"

"I saw them," I say, doing my best to lock the shape of them into my memory. I can't explain why, but somehow, it feels important.

"I guess it's pointless to ask if anyone knows what the heck just happened?" Maritza says.

Enzo returns to the cloak he found in the corner before the crows came. This time, when he picks it up, its pointed beak is easier to see, and I notice something I didn't the first time: a thick tapestry of hundreds of slick black bird feathers.

"I don't know, but I feel like whatever this is might have something to do with it."

Trinity gets closer, examining the beaked hood that reaches long enough to shield a face.

"I'm beginning to think that the Forest Protectors are more people than bird."

I nod, refocusing on the tracks in the floor that no longer glow green and purple.

"Yeah, and I'm guessing whatever they're 'protecting' has less to do with the forest and more to do with whatever just happened here."

"All very fascinating," says Enzo, dropping the cloak, "but did anyone notice that sometime during that little light show, our only passage out of here disappeared?"

We each take a corner of the room, groping around for anything resembling a box or chair to stand on, or a way to hoist ourselves back to the opening, not that we know how to open it. Even Enzo, the tallest among us, can only stretch his arm to touch the bottom seam of the opening.

Maritza scoffs. "How is it none of you has ever made a human pyramid?"

Well, at least one of us is thinking rationally.

Enzo and I reluctantly form the base.

"I don't remember signing up for this tonight," Enzo grumbles.

"There's a lot we didn't sign up for tonight," Maritza snaps back as she climbs on top of our backs.

Enzo doesn't answer. Instead, he mumbles something about Maritza weighing as much as an elephant while Mya climbs on our backs as well, then hoists herself onto Maritza's shoulders, reaching the passage door.

"What do you see?" I ask from the ground.

"A closed door," Mya says.

"Thanks. That's enlightening." I try again. "Something that resembles a handle? A hinge?"

"Would you be quiet? I'm trying to think," Mya says, running her fingers along the outline of the passage door like she's waiting for it to talk to her. It wouldn't be the weirdest thing that's happened tonight.

"By all means, take your time," Enzo says, his voice shaking about as hard as his body is.

"I think a chunk of the wall is permanently part of my knee," I groan, trying to shift my weight.

"If you guys don't hold still—" Maritza warns.

"All of you, be quiet!" Trinity scolds.

"Easy for you to say," says Enzo.

"All of you, hush!" Mya says, then looks down at me. "Aaron, how'd you say you found the passage door in the weather station?"

"Uh, I fell through a hole," I say. "Seems to be a theme."

But I think I see where she's going with this. If the passage was hidden in the weather station, and the passage door in our basement was only opened through a hidden switch . . .

Suddenly, all of Mya's feeling around the walls makes sense.

"Was the switch located in a particular part of the wall?" Mya asks, but I have no idea.

"I just kind of stumbled on it, or through it, or . . ."

"There should be some sort of connection, a place where the switches are placed that's significant somehow."

Mya whips her head around, nearly toppling the pyramid.

"It's where I shocked myself."

I'm struggling to keep up. Everyone else is struggling to keep upright.

"Aaron, where'd you shock yourself?"

I look back at the wall that bit me. "I don't wanna touch it again."

"Well, good news, you can't," Mya says, reminding me I'm the base of the pyramid.

"It's all you, Ms. Supervisor," Enzo says to Trinity.

"I don't want to get shocked, either!"

"Just do it!" Mya hisses.

Trinity begins feeling tentatively around the wall where I was.

Zap!

"Ow! Okay, found it. Happy?"

"Keep feeling around."

"I think I might have something."

A grinding sound echoes through the strange eight-sided room and the passage door slides open.

Mya crawls through first, turning to extend an arm to Maritza. Trinity climbs in next.

I look at Enzo, patting my shoulder and crouching. "Hop on," I say.

"Um," he says. He knows he's stronger than me.

"I'm gonna need you to pull me up," I say, annoyed.

He climbs onto my shoulders awkwardly, and I sway backward, barely catching my balance before bringing us both crashing to the ground.

"If you're trying to kill me, there are easier ways," he snorts.

"I could've just left you down here," I snarl.

"Kids, if you're finished, can we please leave the weird radioactive room and get back to the creepy tunnels?" Trinity scolds.

She pulls Enzo through the opening. They form a chain to hoist me up last.

I take a parting look at the room. I have so many more questions for it.

Mya takes my wrist and pulls me away before sliding the door shut with a press of the lever hidden in the wall.

"The weather station will have answers," she says, reading my mind. "It has to."

"Oh no. No, no, no, no," Enzo says. "Home. We're going home. I've had enough."

"But we didn't even make it to the weath—" I start to protest, but Trinity and Maritza have lined up beside Enzo.

"We've already been down here a long time," Trinity says. "What if someone notices we're gone?"

"What if *your dad* notices?" Maritza says, and I want to resent my dad somehow becoming the villain in this story, but it's getting a little hard to do that. The tunnel door is in *his* office. What might he know about where all the tunnels go? What does he know about this room?

And what does he know about the people wearing cloaks made of feathers that look a lot like what people have been describing for years as Forest Protectors?

"Maybe they're right," Mya says quietly, then leans in to murmur, "We can always come back another night."

She means just her and me.

I'm about to agree when I peer down the tunnel, for the first time seeing it from this perspective. Facing the opposite direction, the bend of the tunnel looks shockingly familiar.

I don't say a word. I don't think anything. All I know— all my body knows—is to *run*.

"Aaron!"

They're calling after me, but it's a mess of echoes in here, and I have no intention of stopping. Not when we're this close. No one can stop me.

When I reach a small passage on my right, I realize we must have passed by it. Coming from the opposite direction, it would have been hard to see the opening unless we had the light shining right on it, which of course we didn't.

"This way!"

"Aaron, slow down! Have you lost it?"

Maybe. Probably. I don't care. This is the way to the weather station. I'm sure of it.

When I hear the rest of them catch up to me, I'm already looking at the passage I dropped from on the day I found the door in the weather station across the hall from my grandparents' office.

"Are you sure?" Mya asks, looking.

"Positive."

Enzo drops to his hands and knees, grimacing at the slime he lands in. "Let's make this fast," he says.

The pyramid forms again, only now it's me this time atop Trinity's shoulders. I find the outline of the passage door fast, but no matter where I press on the wall, the door won't budge. Mya tries the opposite wall to no avail.

"Anyone feeling static electricity?" I ask. Mya and Maritza rub their arms.

"Nothing."

Dropping from Trinity's shoulders, I hang my head and welcome the disappointment I'm beginning to grow used to.

"Do you feel that?" Maritza says, holding her hand in the air, and for a second, I dare to hope. "It's a breeze."

She walks down the dark tunnel.

I follow Maritza as far as I can until I lose sight of her altogether. In fact, I lose sight of everything, which is why I practically run face-first into the wall before I realize the passage has bent sharply to the left. I see Maritza's feet retreating once again into the darkness.

Trinity, Mya, and Enzo close behind, we follow Maritza's lead until we feel the breeze, too. It's mild at first, but soon, the smell of fresh rain from a recent storm fills the narrow tunnel.

Finally, a blue light arcs ahead, shadows of crisscrossing grass and weeds obscuring the bottom half of the opening.

When we've all emerged, it's clear from the faces of my friends and Mya that not a single one of us knows where the heck we are.

"Well, guess we found a way around that whole 'no going into the forest' rule," I say.

"I was okay with that rule," Enzo says.

"All we have to do is look for something familiar," says Trinity. "Like a landmark."

But everything looks exactly the same as the next, from the trees to the underbrush to each blade of grass in this forest. It's like nature is trying to hold us captive.

Mya spots the brick wall first.

"I don't see it," I say, peering through the dark.

"Are you sure that's the same one that surrounds the weather station?" Enzo says.

"How many random brick walls do you suppose there are in the forest?" snipes Mya.

Clearly, we're all getting a little grumpy. I never claimed this midnight mission was a good idea. Or maybe I did. Whatever, there's no going back now.

The closer we get to where Mya was pointing, the clearer it becomes that this is indeed the same wall that extends the perimeter of the weather station, though this particular section of wall looks unfamiliar. I'd always suspected the weather station was big, but the wall looks like it stretches infinitely into the depths of the forest. I can't even see where it bends to form the next side.

BIRDSEED

"Last one to find a way in is—" Mya starts.

"Birdseed?" quips Maritza.

We search high and low for a door, or a hatch, or a manhole. I'd settle for a gutter at this point. I refuse to accept that we could be this close to the weather station after all we've been through tonight and not get in.

"It's a gutter," says Trinity, lip curled.

Indeed it is.

"Is it really that different than crawling through those tunnels?" Mya reasons.

"I don't think it's an *actual* gutter," I say. "Like, not a sewage gutter."

It sure looks like one, though. It's covered by a metal grate, which, luckily or not (depending on who you ask), lifts off with little effort thanks to a couple of loose bolts and good ole weather erosion. Score one for Raven Brooks's wacky weather!

"That makes me feel a ton better," Trinity says.

Enzo extends a hand. "Lead the way."

I guess that's fair. I cast a glance at Mya, who looks only a little more convinced this is a good idea than Trinity does. Then I slide through the opening.

The sludge greases my path through the chute, and I guess I should be grateful. I might be if I didn't want to puke so bad.

"I really liked these jeans," Maritza says, frowning at the streaks of unidentifiable grime along her legs.

"I don't think I'm ever gonna get this smell out of my nose," says Enzo.

We walk for what feels like hours. Maybe that's because we *have* been walking for hours, if you count our journey through the tunnels. By the time we reach the hallway that runs behind the now sealed front door of the weather station, I halfway wonder if it's just a mirage.

When Mya takes the lead, I know it's real.

My grandparents' office is exactly as we left it, almost as though frozen in time.

"Bingo, the rest of the notebook," Mya says, holding the bound bundle of yellowing papers in the air like some important ancient relic.

Then, right on cue, I hear Maritza call from the hallway. "Uh, guys?"

I already know it's bad news before we reach her. Somehow, though, that doesn't keep a strong chill from traveling down my spine at the sight of what she's standing over.

A series of wooden boards hang on the wall by hastily hammered nails, their heads bent under the rush.

"That explains why the door wouldn't open from the tunnel," Enzo says.

Trinity's gaze falls on the small ruffle of black feathers scattered on the ground by the boarded-up door. "And I guess that explains who didn't want us opening it."

"I've seen all I need to," Maritza says, backing away from the feathers.

This time, I couldn't agree more.

We're halfway down the long corridor leading to the gutter before we remember our epic slide down the sludge tube.

"There's no way we're going to be able to climb our way back up that ramp," Trinity says.

"If there's one thing I am positive about," I say, "it's that this place has about a million different doors leading in and out of it. It's like the least fun fun house ever."

"Golden Apples," Enzo says suddenly, his eyes glazing over like so much melted sugar. "Never doubt the nose."

Off he goes like a bloodhound on the trail, keeping his head high in the air. The rest of us have to run to keep up with his long stride.

We pass through corridor after corridor, locked door after locked door. I imagine the secrets each closed door hides and promise myself I'll find out.

Someday. Someday.

With heaving chests, we find ourselves impossibly in front of another tunnel opening.

"Please, no more tunnels," Trinity pleads, but Enzo barrels ahead, his nose an unstoppable force.

It isn't long before things begin to look familiar again.

All that's missing is a blood-streaked wallet and a trail of black feathers.

The smell of saccharine grows stronger and stronger until, at last, Enzo pushes through the door, and we're standing in the middle of the Golden Apple factory basement.

I take a deep breath. Here it is—irrefutable evidence that my grandparents had direct access to the very factory they were suspected of burning down.

It was one thing when just Mya and I knew the bitter truth. It's an entirely different thing when all of our friends can see it firsthand.

"You didn't do anything," Enzo says, reading the shame all over my face.

I know he's trying, and maybe that should make me feel better, only it doesn't.

"I'm all for breathing in the sweet, sweet fumes of Golden Apples," Maritza says, "but I'm not sure how this helps us get back to Aaron and Mya's house."

Mya looks at me. "Think you can remember how to get back to the tree where you saw the nest?"

"From there, it's a straight shot to the construction site. Then we're practically home free," I say.

We don't speak another word as we carefully pick our way through the forest. I try not to pay attention to the way the sky glows blue with the approaching dawn. We've been out all night. If we don't make it back soon, Mom's going to open our doors to a bunch of empty sleeping bags, and, well . . . maybe there *is* something scarier than what we found in the tunnels.

And then we hear emergency sirens.

We all stop.

"The construction road," Trinity whispers, her hand floating to her mouth. "They're headed for the Golden Apple Amusement Park."

Chapter 9

By the time we reach the Golden Apple Amusement Park construction site, the sirens have stopped, but the scene is crawling with more activity than any of us has ever seen.

"Make a hole, people, let him through!"

"I couldn't believe it! One minute he's soldering the track at the top; next he's hanging from his foot like a toy on a string!"

"Where's the lead engineer? We need the lead engineer!"

"Someone get Mayor Tavish on the phone."

"He's coming through! Get the ramp ready!"

Men and women in yellow construction vests cluster together, shaking their heads. Emergency-medical-looking people in blue jumpsuits stand posted at the ambulance while several others maneuver a man on a stretcher through the crowd. The guy on the gurney is making the most noise by far.

"Whaddya mean 'Where does it hurt?' It hurts everywhere! I just fell from the top of a gosh-darn mountain, ya idiot!"

"Sir, try to stay calm."

"Owwwwww! You tryin' to finish me off? Owww!"

With the man inside, the ambulance and a fire truck depart the scene in a massive cloud of dust and exhaust, leaving the site relatively quiet in its wake.

That doesn't mean it's calm, though.

"Tavish is on his way. DEFCON 2."

"Hey, don't look at me. I didn't vote for the guy."

"*Nobody* voted for the guy. Somehow, he still gets to be mayor. Go figure."

"I don't get it. How the heck did Mackey fall from the coaster? Guy wouldn't climb a two-foot ramp without a safety belt!"

"I don't know, but I'm beginning to think folks are right about this place."

"C'mon, Dwayne, not you, too."

"I'm just saying. Three accidents, two acts of vandalism, and a missing security guard. You don't have to be Dick Tracy to crack this case. The place is cursed."

"Heads up. Keith Newsom and his slick detective buddy."

"I don't think they're buddies."

"Where did this guy even come from? Since when does Raven Brooks have a detective?"

The swirls of whispered theories and gossip come to a quick stop when a blue sedan rolls up. Detective Dale and Officer Keith climb out of the car.

I should have caught my breath by now—we've been standing here long enough. I realize after a second it's because I've been holding it pretty much this entire time. By the way Mya and our friends are panting, I'd guess they were doing the same.

Without a word, we slip back into the brush and work our way around the perimeter of the construction site, taking the long way while the detective cuts across the site. I feel like a mouse scurrying through a giant abandoned mansion, sheets covering the furniture and hiding horrible secrets in forgotten rooms.

"I had no idea the park was this big," Trinity whispers as we quickly pick our way through the brush.

But Mya and I aren't surprised. *Fernweh Welt* was almost as big. And if it's anything like the park in Germany— and I'm beginning to think it is—they're leaving one ride as a surprise for the public. It's the centerpiece for the whole park. The gem for reviewers and parkgoers alike. At *Fernweh Welt*, they called it the ride that would make the "biggest splash."

And make a splash it did.

Finally, we reach a wall, except it's not a wall at all. It's some sort of sturdy tarp strung across the length of the park from one side to the other, tied to two tall trees.

They have to be that tall to hold the massive tarp, which is at least three hundred feet high, supported by poles that extend even higher than the tallest points of the supporting trees.

"Oh man, I feel sick just looking at that," Enzo says, his head tilted like an open PEZ dispenser.

As we make our way around the tarp, I feel sick. There's a growing suspicion that whatever is lurking behind this massive canvas wall isn't a thrill ride.

It's a curse.

Nothing could have prepared us for what we see when we emerge on the other side of the tarp.

The coaster starts with a climb so high, clouds might obscure the apex on overcast days. Then comes the drop, an impossibly steep angle that dips to the lowest point in the track before thrusting the chain of cars into a sideways curve, turning in a tight corkscrew as it climbs once again to a double loop-the-loop, snaking back and forth in S-curves designed for maximum disorientation. The ride climbs two more hills at near-vertical slopes before coming to an abrupt stop at its origin point.

It is a roller coaster perfect in its designed terror. A sign emblazoned across the car station reads THE ROTTEN CORE.

"How is that even . . ." Maritza breathes, staring toward the apex with unblinking eyes.

"Possible?" Enzo finishes, equally awestruck.

"It's . . . not," Trinity says, staring at the same point as all of us—that dizzying apex. "I mean, I don't think it is."

"It has to be," Enzo says, then looks to Mya and me. "Right?"

I wait for Mya to say something. Maybe she's waiting for me to answer. Maybe we both know there isn't an answer, not one that would be satisfactory enough. Our friends have said it all already: It shouldn't be possible.

But they don't know our dad.

"Oh, you've got to be kidding me!" Enzo says suddenly—and loudly—enough to earn a shush from each of us. When we see what's got him so bent out of shape, though, it's hard to blame him.

There, beside the wreckage of a huge fallen beam and several damaged pallets of wood, stands Chetbutt Biggbottoms—chest puffed, microphone under his chin, clearing his throat and making a series of bizarre shapes with his mouth as he exaggerates his pronunciation.

"Lily lies limp by the lake. Daphne dances dutifully during dawn. Pepper pickles prunes prior to—"

"Ah, excuse me, Chet? Chet?"

Chettar Cheese stops, his mouth caught in a tiny O, and suddenly, he looks like a giant toddler wearing a suit, holding a foam microphone with a big *4* squared underneath.

He glares down at his little cameraman.

The cameraman shrinks even smaller. "Sorry to interrupt you sir, but—"

"And yet you do. All the time. Every single day of my life."

The cameraman looks down at the ground like his soul might have just spilled into a puddle there. He steps back and allows the tidal wave of rage that's approaching them to rush in unimpeded.

I can hear Mayor Tavish before he's even passed through the tarp.

"How hard is it to pick up the phone? I mean, how hard

is it? I shouldn't be hearing about this from my wife—my wife! Who only heard about it because she's friends with the police dispatcher, and . . . oh, this is great. This is just great!"

He's far away, and I can hardly make out the expression on the mayor's face, but I can see that it's as red as a strawberry. His fists are balled at his sides, and he's swinging his arms like propellers as he rants to no one and everyone. He charges right up to Chet Biggs, pushing past the cameraman and poking the anchor in his puffy chest.

"Now look here, Chet. I don't give a ratatouille about your ratings or your gargantuan ego. This story is not airing. I've got far too much riding on this park. Nothing is going to stop us from opening on time this summer."

"Marv, Marv, Marv." Chet Smalls smiles. "Take a breath, would you? You're gonna pass out if you keep this up!"

"Don't you worry about me, Biggs. Worry about yourself! I'll have you tied up in court proceedings six ways from Sunday if you try putting this story on television!"

"Marv—"

"Marvin," Mayor Tavish growls.

"Marv," Chet-the-Meanie Biggs-Biggsly continues, his smile growing even wider. "It's really not up to me," he says, and he is the absolute worst at faking sincerity. I don't think he's even trying.

"Is that so?" Mayor Tavish challenges, but I can see from here that he falters.

"If you have an issue with our coverage, I suggest you take it up with Gordon."

On cue, a tall man in a brown suit steps out of the Channel Four satellite van, gnawing toothpick wriggling between his teeth. He talks around it.

"Marv, sorry you felt the need to rush down here. We've got it under control."

The news director leans against the Channel Four van examining something in his fingernails. He doesn't bother looking at the mayor.

"It's Marvin, and in case you've forgotten, I'm the mayor of Raven Brooks."

"Nobody's forgotten, Marv," says the news director. He sounds positively exhausted, which only makes Mayor Tavish grow redder. I swear, he's going to ignite into a ball of fire in a second. What I can't understand is why no one seems to be worried that he's angry. Not the tiny cameraman. Certainly not the station manager.

"Gordon, be reasonable. You know this can't be broadcast."

Mayor Tavish steps closer to the station manager, who looks at the mayor like he's a bug he can't get away from.

"We're talking about my reputation here," the mayor mumbles, and it actually sounds like he's . . . begging.

The news manager takes a reluctant step toward Mayor Tavish and leans close to him, cupping a hand on his shoulder before patting the mayor's cheek.

"We'll use a soft touch, okay, Marv?"

"Gordon, please, you have to—"

Suddenly, the station manager grows stern. "We don't *have* to do anything."

Then, with his eyes searing into Mayor Tavish's, he says so quietly I have to strain to hear it, "You had your time. It's my turn now. So be a good boy, and back off."

If the station manager had a rolled-up newspaper, I wouldn't have been surprised to see him slap Mayor Tavish's nose with it. Mayor Tavish takes a step back, allowing the station manager to quietly collect himself. Then the manager closes the door on Mayor Tavish without so much as a goodbye.

And without any parting words of his own, Mayor Tavish stomps back the way he came, past the news crew and confused construction workers. Only this time, the mayor looks as white as the tarp obscuring the roller coaster from the rest of the park.

Chetfart Biggtoots returns to his verbal exercises. He looks like he's about to throw a tantrum.

"Mr. Biggs?" says the cameraman, cowering.

Chet McFace sighs the deepest of sighs. "Yes?"

"It's just that the detective is here, and—"

That's when the weirdest thing happens.

Chetty Biggity turns toward the approaching Detective Dale and Officer Keith, and even though Officer Keith is charging ahead like he hates Chet almost as much as

Enzo does, Detective Dale puts his arm in front of Officer Keith to block him. Maybe it's my imagination on over-drive, but I'd swear I see Chet Biggburps and Detective Dale exchange a nod.

And then Detective Dale just steps to the side and lets Chet do his report from the spot where some guy practi-cally just fell to his death *before* the police even examine the scene.

"How?" Enzo continues to rail. "How could Channel Four have gotten the story this fast. The guy *just* fell like two seconds ago!"

"Enzo, *be quiet!*" Trinity scolds, pushing him closer to the ground and prompting us all to do the same. The brush here is thicker than it had been at the front of the park, but it would still take just one wrong move for everyone to know we're here snooping.

"Okay, but seriously, am I the only one seeing this?" Enzo whispers, exasperated. And the thing is, he's not the only one seeing it. That's not what's bothering me, though.

What's bothering me is that my dad is seeing it, too.

I didn't believe it was him at first. Like everything else that's happened tonight, it didn't seem real, not at first.

I thought I saw his broad-shouldered shadow peeking out from behind a pile of rebar toward the front of the park when we first arrived. But then the medics zoomed in with the guy on the gurney, and when they passed, he was gone. Nothing by the rebar but a crooked tree.

It wasn't until Detective Dale strolled up to Chet Biggs that I saw him again. And this time, there was no mistaking him.

There was my dad, almost completely obscured behind a circular ride draped in the same mysterious tarp every other attraction is hidden under. Just standing there as still as the trees that hide him, taking in the same scene we are.

Only I have no idea why.

As though sensing my question, he shifts his gaze, and suddenly, my dad is staring straight at me, across the grounds of the park he's created.

I don't know if my dad slipped away when I blinked, or my lack of sleep is finally catching up with me, but suddenly, the place where he was is empty. It's like my dad was never there.

"Guys?" Maritza says, and something in her tone finally makes me break my gaze from across the park, returning to our fugitive party of five.

Only we're not five anymore. We're only four.

"Where's—?" Maritza starts to say. Only I finish her sentence.

"My sister?"

Chapter 10

"**M**ya? Mya!"

"She couldn't have gone far," Trinity reasons, but it doesn't exactly comfort me that she looks so worried.

I can't help myself. I take off in a sprint, but it's not like I have any idea of where I'm going. I can hardly put together a single coherent thought.

All I know is that Mya was there a second ago, and now she's not, and too much has happened tonight and this morning for me to feel like any part of Raven Brooks is safe.

"Mya!" I call out.

I'm darting from tree to tree like I expect to see her crouched in one.

My friends catch up to me and follow my lead, but none of us knows what to do.

"This was a mistake," I say, falling against a tree and squeezing my head between my hands.

"What was a mistake?"

"All of it. Just all of it," I say.

Then I realize it was Mya's voice asking me.

She's on the other side of the tree that caught me in my fall toward despair.

As I round the trunk, I go to grab her by her shoulders and shake her or hug her or drag her back home when I notice that she isn't looking at me or Trinity or Enzo or Maritza. She's looking straight up.

When I follow her gaze, I'm speechless.

Enzo is not.

"Chet Biggs is gonna be mad he missed this," he says.

"Okay, now I really wish I had my camera," Trinity says.

We don't debate it. We don't have to. We already know one of us is going to have to climb the tree.

Nestled high in the branches of this particular tree, this very evil tree, is a nest big enough to fit a person-sized bird.

Enzo volunteers to climb it since he's tallest, but somewhere, deep down, we all know it's got to be me. I've come in close contact with this trunk before. And it's my grandparents who (maybe) were involved. It's me. It's gotta be me.

No human pyramid necessary this time, I jump on the lowest branch. If I had much memory of that day I fell out of the tree, I might be a little wary this time around, but most of that day feels like it was a dream. I wonder how much of this night and morning will feel the same.

The second and third branch are fairly easy to reach. I hoist myself to each level, barely rattling the leaves of the tree. The next branch, though—that one's a doozy.

I look down at my friends and sister for guidance, but all they can do is shrug.

"Thanks for the confidence," I mumble, trying twice to reach the branch from my tiptoes. But it's no use. I need about six more inches.

I'm going to have to jump for it.

I look down again. Maybe it's not as far as it looked a second ago. But nope. It is.

I remind myself how close we are to finally finding some answers. The nest might hold nothing at all—or it might hold the key to whatever missing piece of this bonkers puzzle we've been looking for.

What I know for sure is that we won't get another chance at finding a nest. In my gut, I know it.

"One," I breathe.

It's probably not as far away as it looks.

"Two."

Bright side: I already know how falling feels.

"Three."

I didn't mean to close my eyes, and in hindsight it was kind of stupid because what was I supposed to do, *imagine* my way to the branch?

Except whatever I did must have worked because I'm swinging from it right now, and whatever miracle that saved me from plunging to my death has also given me branch-swinging superpowers, probably.

Then I'm directly underneath the nest.

It's so massive, I realize I'm actually going to have to climb out on the branch underneath it just to see over the edge. Right now, it's looming over my head like a saucer, and actually, it wouldn't surprise me to find a little green man hanging out in there. It might be a relief over seeing a Forest Protector.

"There's no Forest Protector in there," I reassure myself.

Of course there isn't. Because they're not really birds, and they don't actually live in nests, waiting patiently for some stupid kid to climb right into their treetop home before they drain him of all his blood and offer him up to their bird overlord. I'm mostly convinced that the rumors have it all wrong.

Mostly.

"Keep it together, Peterson," I mutter. Then I close my eyes and say it once more. "Keep it together."

I keep my eyes closed as I lift myself onto the branch, perching like a . . . well, bird.

Then I open my eyes.

The nest isn't a nest at all. Not really. It has the makings of a nest—the interwoven twigs and branches and dried leaves, tall blades of grass that act as threads connecting the whole mess together.

Now that I'm in front of it, *really* seeing the thing for the first time, it's less impressive than I thought it would be. Sure, it's huge—probably the circumference of our dining room table—but it doesn't look sturdy enough to hold a large bird, let alone a human-sized one. To test my theory, I carefully take one hand from my supporting branch and grasp it, shaking it a little from side to side. Sure enough, it moves easily, unsettling the bundles of twigs and brush enough to nearly break apart.

"It's all just a big fake-out," I say to myself, surprised at how betrayed I feel. It's like it's all a ruse to keep people believing in the Forest Protectors. "But why?"

Then I spot something else I shook loose, something that's tumbled directly to the middle of the nest.

It's not quite round, but not a cube, either. It has lots of sides, each one catching the early dawn light creeping past the clouds. From here, it looks to be about the size of my palm, a tarnished brassy thing utterly out of place amid the leaves and branches.

I lean closer but don't dare put any weight on the flimsy nest. Instead, I wiggle the edge again, hoping to jostle the object closer.

It works.

I shake again, and again, the brass thing—it has even more sides than I thought, eight maybe, kind of like the creepy room earlier, actually—skitters a little closer. I keep at it until finally the object is within reach. I'm so close, I think it's safe to take another step, but I fail to see the hairline fracture in the branch I'm standing on.

The branch cracks, and my hand slips from the support. I scramble to grasp something for support but miss. It's sheer luck that the branch below catches me.

Right in the gut.

"Ugggggghhhh." I hang there like a sloth for I don't know how long, but long enough for the wind to return to my lungs and my hip bone to be super angry with me. Punctuating my fall, the nest finally comes apart.

I climb carefully down the rest of the way, landing with an ungraceful thud on the ground before turning to find my friends and sister. They're picking pieces of nest out of their hair and clothes.

"That's one way to hide the evidence," Mya says, unraveling a thorny twig from her hair.

I immediately start scrambling through the fallen nest pieces in search of the brass whatever-it-is.

"This . . . doesn't look like an egg," Trinity says.

I turn to find her holding the object, and soon, we're crowded in a tight circle staring at her open palm.

On closer inspection, it does have eight sides, and though they're dingy, I can easily spot the grooves carved deep into the surface. It's heavier than I expected it to be, too, almost the weight of a can of soup. A tiny ridge along one of its eight sides resembles a hinge, but no amount of turning the object over and over again reveals a means of opening the box.

* * *

Trinity closes her hand around it and shakes. The box rattles.

"There's something in there," she says, then shakes again with her hand closer to her ear.

Whatever the box is, I can't seem to stop staring at it. There's something almost ancient-looking about it, with its tarnished bronze and intricate grooves. Yet, something tells me there's much more to this than a box holding a trinket inside.

Suddenly, footfalls at the edge of the construction site begin crunching deeper into the forest.

"I daresay His Royal Highness Mayor Tavish has forgotten who's really in charge," I hear a deep, gravelly voice say, and immediately, we dive for cover behind the nearest snarl of overgrowth.

"Eh, don't worry about Marv," I hear Detective Dale say. "He's just enjoying his moment in the sun."

"It's not his moment anymore," says the gravelly voice, and there it is, that undercurrent of warning—not quite a threat, but it sure is close. Detective Dale is talking to the Channel Four station manager.

"Nobody's gonna take your turn, Gordon," says Detective Dale, sounding tired. He's starting to lose some of his trademark cool.

Maybe I'm starting to lose some of my mind because I risk a peek at the men huddled at the edge of the tree line, and what I see chills me to my core.

Gordon Cleave gets so close to Detective Dale's face, I actually see the detective look frightened for the very first time. He takes a step back, and Gordon Cleave leans closer.

"That's right, Dale. Nobody's going to take my turn.

Because we know what happens when the cycle gets broken, don't we?"

I don't know how long they stay locked in their stare, or how long I stay locked in their locked stare, or how long Enzo tugs on my shirt in an effort to break my trance and get me to follow the rest of them the heck out of there, but however long it was, I know I'll be having nightmares about that interaction for a long time. And that's saying a lot given the night we've had.

We creep back through the open basement door of the Golden Apple factory and descend the stairs back into the tunnels.

We hardly talk on the way. There's so much to say, and yet none of us knows how to say it. We came here looking for answers, but all we're leaving with are more questions.

What was all that talk about "my turn" and "breaking the cycle"?

What if my dad's been watching this whole thing unfold? Exactly how much does he know?

And what does that mean for Forest Protectors? For Mya and me?

"What was that?" I say, stopping suddenly enough that Enzo runs into my back. Trinity, Mya, and Maritza spin around, looking to the sides while I look behind me.

"What was what?"

"I heard something," I say, my chest sore from all the

pounding my heart's been doing over the past few hours.

We're still for another minute, but aside from the occasional drip of water, nothing echoes through the tunnels.

"There's nothing there, Aaron," Maritza says carefully, like my brain is fragile. Maybe it is. Maybe this is what it feels like to crack up.

The rest of the walk through the tunnels is completely silent. The entire time, I try to shake the feeling that we're being followed.

When we finally reach the passage back to our basement, I feel like we've just emerged through a wormhole. Nothing in my dad's study looks the same as it did when we left. Maybe it's the breaking daylight that's trying to seep in through the windowless room. Or maybe it's the burning in my eyes from lack of sleep.

All I know is that somehow, beyond all reason and probability, Enzo and I make it back up to my room, and Trinity, Maritza, and my sister make it back to her room, with exactly seven minutes to spare before I hear my parents' bedroom door creak open, my mom's feet shuffling in her slippers down the stairs, and the timer on the stove starting so that she can make the pancakes she promised us for the morning.

"We did it," Enzo says, grinning at me from the bottom bunk as I hang my head over the side of the top.

"What do you think?" I ask him.

"About which part?"

I shrug and shake my head slowly. "All of it."

He shakes his head back, but the weight of the night is still settling, and we both seem to understand that we've crossed a line somehow. We can't go back to not knowing anymore—about the Forest Protectors and their nests, about the tunnels and the weather station, the observatory and its weird glowing lights, the copper box we still can't manage to open.

Was this all a grave mistake?

* * *

Apparently, sneaking through underground tunnels and braving strange electrical storms works up quite the appetite because Mom can hardly pour the batter in the pan fast enough to make enough pancakes for five ravenous mouths.

"Yikes, you kids are hungrier than Ted on a late-night work binge," she says. "That man can clean out a fridge so fast, you'd think a bear got in the house overnight. Speaking of your father, have you kids seen him this morning?"

If Mom wasn't paying such close attention to flipping the next cake, she would have seen me practically choke on my orange juice. And if I hadn't been looking across the table at just that moment, I would have missed Mya catching my eye, and in that blink-and-you'd-miss-it second, I know that I wasn't the only one who witnessed my dad at the site of the accident this morning.

"Haven't seen him," Mya says to my mom, never taking her eyes from me.

"Nope," I agree, unblinking.

I finally blink away from Mya and consider how differently this morning could have gone. Who knew the line between syrup and a lifetime of being grounded was so razor-thin?

With sleeping bags rolled and pajamas smashed into backpacks, Enzo, Trinity, and Maritza take their leave, but not before a quick pact is made out of earshot of Mom.

"We'll start scouring the archives at the *Banner* for any mention of that . . . box thingy," Maritza says, and Enzo nods.

"I'll see if I can get anything out of Mrs. Ryland. Lucy's in the Storm Chasers, and I'll tag along to their next club and pretend to be interested."

And then they're off, our coconspirators in a scandal I never wanted but now can't seem to get out of.

After we help Mom with the dishes, Mya nudges my shoulder.

"My room," she says, rinsing the last dish.

In Mya's room, I roll the brass object back and forth in my hands while we scour the collection of torn pages and bound notes from our grandparents.

"I thought this would make more sense after we got a closer look at their research, but seriously, it's like an entirely different language," I say, carefully uncurling the crunchy, weathered pages with writings belonging to people I'm wishing more and more I'd known before they died.

Maybe it's me hoping they're innocent. But the more we read through their frantic scrawling, the more I begin to suspect they weren't responsible for the weirdness around Raven Brooks.

"I mean, what are we supposed to make of this?" Mya agrees, shoving one particularly frenetic set of scratchings in front of me.

Somewhere in the midst of long, complicated formulas that seem to stretch half the length of the page, various circles and arrows seem to offer warnings or epiphanies or . . . brain farts. I have no idea.

"What does 'fractals inverted' even mean?" Mya says, rubbing her head like it hurts.

"I'll see your 'inverted fractals' and raise you one 'reverse evapotranspiration,'" I say.

I push the pages away, feeling more hopeless than ever. "This is never going to make sense. Why couldn't this be about art? Art makes sense to me."

That's when it dawns on me. Why the brass box seemed so familiar.

"Mya, we need to get back down to the basement," I say, and I must look completely possessed because she actually scoots away from me a little on the carpet.

"Not back in the tunnels," she says, her arms pinned over her chest. "Nope. Not doing it."

"No. We just need to get to Dad's study."

Mya looks at me like I've grown a tail. Maybe I have. It's been a long night.

"Just trust me," I say.

Downstairs, Mom is crashed out on the couch.

"You kids . . . need anything?" she asks without lifting her head. I can only see her ponytail, curled over the arm of the sofa, her body limp across the cushions. I wonder if she's this exhausted from making us all breakfast. She couldn't possibly be worried about Dad . . . could she?

"Nope!" I say, and I swear she actually lets out one little sob of relief.

"Okay, then," she says, and now I understand where I get my terrible talent at faking it.

"Just gonna . . . go exploring," Mya says, and I jab her in the ribs with my elbow, which earns me a death stare from Mya, but Mom doesn't even flinch.

"Have fun."

We open the basement door as quietly as we can, creeping down the steps like the criminals we are.

"What if Dad's down there?" Mya whispers.

"I think we both know he isn't."

She doesn't say a word.

Sure enough, the basement study is just as we left it only hours earlier—empty.

"What was so important that we had to come down here?" Mya says.

"It's got to be here somewhere," I say, riffling through my dad's blueprints on his desk like he wouldn't eat me for dinner if he found out.

"Maybe if you shared with me what it is you're looking for instead of muttering to yourself like a loon, I could help," Mya says.

"If there's something I never forget, it's a drawing," I

say, and finally, by the same unlikely miracle that saved me from face-planting on the forest floor under the nest this morning, I find it—the drawing on ancient-looking paper that is definitely not in my dad's handwriting but looks an awful lot like it came from the same notebook we just snuck away from the weather station.

I unfurl it. It's a detailed diagram of the very eight-sided box I found in the tree, complete with one very complicated formula that appears to reveal the secret of how to open it.

"Great!" says Mya. "All we need to do is crack this completely impossible code, and we'll be able to see the prize inside! Ooh, maybe if we're lucky, it's a yo-yo!"

I want to be annoyed with her sarcasm, but honestly, I'm too tired to call her on it. And I'm feeling the same hopelessness *so hard*.

"Why? *Why* would we be dragged along this far just to come to another dead end?" I say, and I know it's stupid and careless and a bad idea in a thousand different ways, but I throw the brass box on the ground in abject frustration because what else can I do?

Then it pops open.

Mya and I stare at it for far too long before she finally beats me to the punch, diving for it and palming the box that isn't a box at all.

It's some sort of . . .

"Machine?" she says.

"Device?" I say.

There it is, the inner workings of this container that reveal every single cog and screw and wire and antenna diagrammed in my grandparents' drawing.

"Aaron, I think this is a kind of sensor," Mya says, flipping through the crimped pages of the notebook.

"A weather sensor," I say, and finally, the veil is starting to lift. Maybe, just maybe, this device is starting to make sense.

"Except . . . why?" Mya says.

She's right. What's the big secret? Okay, it's a weather sensor. Why would anyone go to such lengths to hide what's basically a tiny weather balloon?

I sigh. "It's official. I'm more confused than ever."

The front door above us slams shut, making Mya and me flinch. We both look up instinctively, hearing voices come from upstairs.

"There you are," Mom says, and even with a floor separating us, I can tell she's irritated. "You look terrible."

Dad. She doesn't even bother to ask him where he's been. She knows by now she won't get a direct answer.

Dad grunts some sort of response, and then Mom's voice changes.

"Ted, are you okay?"

Grunt. That's Dad's response. Mom seems to understand what he means, though.

"Would you at least eat something first?" Mom pleads, and her voice has softened back to its usual forgiveness. I swear the woman has superhuman patience.

"I managed to wrestle a few pancakes away from the beasts this morning. I barely escaped with my life," she says, and for the first time in what seems like years, I hear Dad chuckle.

Mom's the only one who could make that happen.

When we hear their footsteps retreat to the kitchen, Mya and I know this is our chance.

"Now!" I say, and we scurry out of the office, pulling the door closed behind us. We look convincingly casual as we wander up the stairs to our rooms.

"Tired. Taking a nap!" I call toward the kitchen.

"Up all night?" Mom says.

I laugh nervously. "Comic books weren't gonna read themselves," I call over my shoulder before pounding up the stairs.

"If I wasn't so tired, I'd tell you what a terrible liar you are," Mya whispers, swaying in her bedroom doorway.

"Thanks for sparing my feelings," I scowl, heading for my own room.

"G'night," Mya says, even though the sun is streaming in through her window.

"Good night," I say.

* * *

I'm not kidding. I really do take a long nap. When I open my eyes again, it's dark in my room.

The house is quiet and still.

But not entirely still. Not entirely quiet. Something woke me up.

I sit up in bed and strain my ears for whatever pulled me from sleep fast enough to make my heart thump like this.

Nothing's out of place in my room that I can see. Just a

folding snack table tucked beside my desk with a sandwich and a glass of water. I must have slept through dinner. I slept the entire day away.

Suddenly, I hear it—a thump. Loud enough to be heard but faint enough to be far away.

I lower myself from my bunk as quietly as I can and open my door, waiting for the sound again. Another thump, this one softer than the last, but I know exactly where it's coming from.

The basement.

I'm not sure if I'm mad at Mya for risking going down there after we almost got caught today or going down there without me, but either way, she's gonna get an earful.

Except Mya's bedroom door is cracked open, and there she is, lying sound asleep, an identical untouched sandwich waiting by her bedside. What's going on?

I inch farther down the hallway and peer into my parents' room, but I can hear their alternating snores before I even see into their bedroom.

Whoever is making that sound in the basement isn't someone who should be in this house.

This is the exact moment I should leap onto my parents' bed and warn them that there may be an intruder in the house. This is the very moment when I should yank the phone from its base and dial the police for help.

And I would. I would do all those things if this weren't also the precise moment when I remember that I left the brass device in my father's basement study, along with all of my grandparents' notes and every other bit of evidence we collected in our night of truancy.

I can see it unfolding so clearly:

Dad, Mom, come quick! I think I heard something in the basement! Oh, no one's here. Must have been my imagination. What's this? How did these long-lost items from Grandma and Grandpa's office get here? Ahem, funny story . . .

So, I have two choices: I can go down and investigate myself, or I can wait for Dad to find what we left and face the wrath of sneaking out.

It's really not even a choice, even though my pounding heart might disagree.

My feet are actually sore from all the tiptoeing I've done in the past twenty-four hours. I am officially a delinquent.

"Beat yourself up later. Right now . . ." I say, trying to gather my courage, but I think I might have spent my entire supply because I can't seem to keep my legs from shaking as I descend the stairs.

When I reach the basement door, I realize that I haven't heard the thumping at all since leaving my room, and this feels like it could be a good sign.

"Could've been a dream," I whisper to myself.

More like a waking nightmare.

"Unhelpful," I scold myself and open the door as quietly as I can, but it still squeaks.

I don't dare risk turning on a light, so I have to feel my way to the bottom, then down the long, dark hallway to Dad's study. Still, no sound emerges from the tiny room at the end of the corridor, and by the time I reach the open door of the office, I almost have myself convinced that the sound was all in my head.

Except . . . didn't Mya and I close the door when we left this morning?

I peer into the darkness that cloaks my dad's study. All I have to do is reach around the wall and flip on the light switch. It seems so simple.

Except that the longer I stand in the breathless darkness, the more convinced I am that I'm not standing there alone.

I do my best not to breathe. My muscles are twitching, but I hold my position. I wait. It's the longest wait of my life.

Then a shadow from the farthest corner of the room swells, and it takes everything in me not to scream.

I wait to see what it does. It might lunge for me, and then what would I do?

I should scream. But would that even matter? I'm already down here, three steps away from someone who does not belong here.

I open my mouth to scream anyway. No sound comes out.

Then the shadow makes a sideways movement, and my heart stops. Instead of coming toward me, though, I hear a small sliding sound, and I know that the passage door has opened.

The shadow shrinks back down, and with another sliding sound, I'm suddenly alone in the study once again.

Movement floods into my limbs before my brain starts functioning. My hand flips the light switch, suddenly bringing the room to life. My legs sprint to the end of the room and throw my entire body against the passage door to make absolutely certain it's closed. Then, mustering some sort of superhuman strength, I choose the nearby bookshelf stuffed full of thick tomes and muscle it inch by inch in front of the passage door.

By the time I'm done, I'm sweating and shaking uncontrollably, and my heart refuses to slow down.

After a long while, I finally calm down, but the calm only lasts for a second. When I search the floor for the notes and the device, I see that only the notes remain.

The device is gone.

Chapter 11

My dad made amusement parks before *Fernweh Welt*, but I was too little to remember. In Germany, though, I watched every corner of the park unfold. I saw the spark of possibility ignite in Dad's eye when we first saw it. I felt the rush of creativity radiate off his skin like a current each time he sunk into a ride design. Mom would watch him with quiet delight. She'd seen it a dozen times before, she said, but each time was like the first. It was the same way she felt when she danced, she told me. I understood; that's how it was when I drew.

I felt the shift instantly when it all changed. Suddenly, the spark of possibility smoldered to a dark char. The current running through Dad's veins was still electric, but more like a live wire. He was angry all the time. Explosive, almost. It was dangerous to get too close.

We kept our distance. Mom kept Mya and me out of the house longer, finding adventures to pass the daylight hours after school. At night, Mya and I would lie awake listening to the pencil scratching and angry muttering coming from the kitchen, my dad's only space to work in our small apartment.

The change was impossible to ignore.

Days before the opening of *Fernweh Welt*, we wanted to be excited. That delicious anticipation, where had it gone?

Where had our dad gone?

When it all went wrong with the flume ride, we all wanted to be surprised.

It would have been so much better to be surprised.

Instead, Mom, Mya, and I breathed a collective breath of something that felt like . . . calm. Like the storm that had been building for months had finally arrived, breaking through the atmosphere with deadly vengeance. It was an unthinkable tragedy. Maybe, though, it was finally over.

How Dad felt, we could only guess. He was like a ghost in those days afterward, taking phone calls that were mostly just him listening, saying, "I understand," then hanging up, and sleeping in ten-minute bursts, staring for hours at the same striped wallpaper while Mom hurried to help us understand the inexplicable.

And then we arrived in Raven Brooks.

Which brought us to this morning. When the Golden Apple Amusement Park is scheduled to open on a perfect, cloudless summer day.

Our house is full of activity but utterly silent. Mom is fussing with her outfit and it all feels so familiar.

When we file into the kitchen for a quick breakfast, we see Dad already there, sitting at the table with his hands folded like a student, staring at flowered wallpaper.

"Cripes, Ted, you scared me!" Mom says, but to be fair, a sleeping puppy might have scared her this morning, she's so on edge.

Then we're quiet as we all take a closer look at Dad.

I haven't seen him for days. I've assumed it's because he's been spending all of his time downstairs in his basement study, but looking him over now, it's just as likely he's been sleeping in a warm gutter.

He looks to the side of one wall intently, as if he's following it or sees something there. His eyes twitch ever so slightly. His pants are sweat-stained. His shoes are scuffed and spattered with dried mud.

"We have to leave in five minutes!" my mom says frantically, her eyes seemingly searching for the parts of him she can fix in that time.

"Don't go," Dad says quietly, never taking his eyes from the wall.

"What?" Mom says, her voice finding new heights.

"Please don't go," Dad says just as quietly, just as flatly, as though the only thing missing from his first request was the "please."

"Ted, if this is a joke, we really don't have time."

"It's not a joke."

Mya and I look at each other.

"Kids, go wait in the living room," Mom says, and we don't argue.

I'm not sure why she made us leave, though, because she's even louder than when we were standing right there next to her.

"Don't do this, Ted. You have to keep it together. Just get through today."

"It's happening again," Dad says.

My legs grow weak, and I sink into the couch so Mya can't see them shaking.

"No, it's not," Mom says. "It's your imagin—"

"It's happening," Dad says forcefully, the first inflection

179

I've heard from him this morning. "All I'm asking is that you and the kids stay home. Just stay home," he adds, and the way he says it this time is so disturbing, Mya has to sit down, too.

Because he isn't just asking us not to go to Opening Day. He's begging us.

"Listen to me," Mom says, her voice firm, almost scolding. "You know as well as I do this is nonnegotiable. Marvin Tavish specifically requested the entire family today. He wants his press and he wants his fame, and you and your smiling family are a part of that. He's made it very clear that *we* are all part of the package."

"Diane, you're not listen—"

"No, *you're* not listening. This job has to lead to another, Ted. It *has* to."

Her voice drops from glass-breaking level and switches immediately back to Mom, the woman who would fight a tiger to protect her family.

"I heard back from the bank yesterday. They turned down our loan request. Apparently, washed-up dancers aren't a sound investment for a small business."

Dad is silent for a moment, but I peek into the kitchen and see his hand close over Mom's.

"They're fools," Dad says, and the strangest thing happens. For a single second, he's Dad again. Dad who used to let me draw on his fancy paper. Dad who would watch

Mom in secret while she absently pointed and flexed her toes on the sofa beside him. Dad who painstakingly braided Mya's hair for picture day because Mom's braids never held.

It only lasts for that second, though. We have to leave soon, and Mom doesn't have time to argue.

"They *are* fools, but we're not, Ted," she says firmly. "We're smart. And we have to keep being smart. We have to do what that little twerp wants us to do so he'll ask you to do more. And what he wants is for us all to be there today, holding your hand. Nothing is going to happen."

She says it one more time so Dad will believe it.

Mya can't seem to sit still any longer, and she storms into the kitchen to side with Mom.

"I told all my friends I'd be there," she says.

Dad turns his gaze to me. I don't know what to say. All I can do is shrug. I can't tell if he wants me to side with him or not. I can't tell anything about him anymore.

In the end, Mom wins. I think she was destined to win from the beginning. I think Dad knew that, too. Like everything else leading up to today, it seemed inevitable.

* * *

The road to the Golden Apple Amusement Park has been cleared and paved seemingly overnight. A vast parking lot has been installed, with gleaming white squares drawn for every car in Raven Brooks. I've never seen more balloons. They're tied to every surface, and some weird science has made them apple-shaped. Dad finds a parking spot after some effort, but not before noticing that the VIP spots reserved near the entrance have already been filled by fancier cars and one very large Channel Four satellite van.

I feel a flicker of sympathy for Enzo. Then for me. Why, I'm not yet sure.

The park is still a half hour from opening, but there's

evidence that people literally camped overnight for their place at the front of the line. Haggard-looking parents and teenagers amped on caffeine occupy the front of the line, sleeping bags and tents parked beside them as they shift their weight impatiently.

Behind the sealed entrance, there's enticing hints of what's to come peeking out over the doors: the top crescent of a Ferris wheel, the sound of a nearby carousel cranking out music, the flag perched and waving from a big-top tarp. Then, of course, there's the sweet, sweet aroma of Golden Apples on the air. It smells so delicious, I want to bite into it, taste the air.

All signs point to an epic opening day.

Dad looks even worse under the harsh light of day. In the dimly lit kitchen, I hadn't noticed the dark rings under his eyes, the grime settled into the creases of his palms, the dirt under his nails. He doesn't look self-conscious, though.

He looks terrified.

Mayor Tavish is standing atop a cement box that's part of the sidewalk barrier at the front of the park, no doubt answering Chettina Biggstupid's riveting questions. With the box's assistance, Mayor Tavish and the news anchor are nearly the same height, which I'm sure was no accident. He's ridiculously overdressed amid the summer crowd in his tuxedo, complete with tails and a silver-topped cane. He looks like a lion tamer.

When he sees us approach, he forgets himself and hops

down from the block while still being filmed and hustles over to pull Dad into an aggressive handshake. He's talking louder than usual, as though he thinks the camera can't pick up sound.

"And here he is, the man of the hour!" Mayor Tavish says. "Well, one of the men," he chuckles, pulling at his tux.

A *modest* lion tamer.

"Ah, yes," Chetty Biggsity says in his Chetburps Biggbelches voice, like he's trying to hold in a burp. His cameraman scampers after him as they make their way toward my dad, who doesn't like being on camera even when he's in a good mood.

"Mr. Theodore Peterson," Cheesey Biggface says, moving to place his hand on my dad's sizable shoulder before appearing to think better of it and pulling away. "Can you tell us what some of your inspiration was for this latest creation of yours?"

Dad looks at Chet the same way he looks at him on TV—like the remote control is too far away, but it might just be worth getting up for.

"No," Dad says, and I see Mayor Tavish stiffen.

Mom slides up beside Dad and links an arm through his for support.

Dad clears his throat and leans toward the microphone like he's getting ready to sniff it. "No doubt the, er, Golden Apples. They're . . . uh . . ."

Divine.

Otherworldly.

An adventure for the taste buds.

C'mon, Dad, just say something. Anything.

"Good," he says.

Anything other than "good."

Chetopher Biggsoda chuckles and recovers quickly. "Well, I think we can all rest assured that your park will be better than 'good,' Mr. Peterson. Thanks for taking the time to chat with us."

Chet may be a stink fly of a human, but he's a professional, I'll give him that.

He babbles a little more and deflects Mayor Tavish's offer for more airtime before commanding his cameraman to wrap it up, signing a few autographs for people in the crowd, and retreating to the Channel Four van. When he opens the door, I glimpse Gordon Cleave, looming inside. Which wouldn't be so odd except I'd swear I also see Detective Dale lounging in a seat toward the back of the van.

Before I can get a closer look, the van door slams shut, and all of us, including the cameraman, are left to wait in the growing heat.

Mayor Tavish takes his leave as well, but not without a parting message to Dad.

"Glad you could make it, Ted. Truly. Though I gotta admit. It would have been nice if you, ah, cleaned yourself up a little."

He looks my dad over with his lips pinched before turning on his heel, tuxedo tails flapping in his wake.

"He's like a sour penguin," my mom says as she watches him waddle away.

I love my mom.

A general rumble begins to burble through the crowd, and it doesn't take me long to find the source of unrest.

Moving in a V like a flock of birds, Enzo, Mya, Trinity, Maritza, and Lucy are nudging their way through the massive line at the entrance to the chorus of grumbles and a few outright commands to find the back of the line.

"Calm down, people!" Maritza hollers over the griping. "We're with the family!"

"You make it sound like we're the Mafia," Mya says, hugging her friends.

"Mari and Trin told me everything," Lucy says, wasting zero time. "Who could have taken it?"

I'm not ready to think about the stolen device yet, or the chilling reality of someone being in our basement who absolutely didn't belong there, or the fact that my dad hasn't breathed a word to me or Mya about the moved bookshelf in his study, or the events of that entire delirious night in the tunnels.

"I don't know," I say, and I hope she stops there. I already feel completely horrible for losing the most important—albeit baffling—piece of information from our truant night.

I can't shake the feeling that the device was the real prize. My suspicion is only confirmed by the fact that someone risked sneaking into our house to take it back.

Lucy is kind, though, and she puts her small hand on my arm.

"Cheer up. We get to barf our guts up on that bonkers roller coaster your dad built. It's not all bad!"

Oh, joy. I'd forgotten about the Rotten Core.

Channel Four didn't, though. Sometime in the space of when my friends barged their way through the restless crowd, Chetter Biggsfour, Gordon Cleave, and Detective Dale had exited the van and climbed over the velvet rope blocking the entrance.

"On their way to snag their exclusive," I grumble.

But when I turn to Enzo, expecting an equally glum response, I see him smiling alongside Maritza instead. Maritza's holding back a giddy laugh.

"What? What am I missing?"

"It's the weirdest thing. The *Banner* got an anonymous tip yesterday that the park was unveiling a monster roller coaster on Opening Day," Enzo says, grinning.

"I think it's running in today's edition," Maritza says. "Wacky, right?"

We all turn to watch the Channel Four crew try sneaking off discreetly toward their nonexclusive. I want to relish this petty victory, I really do. But there's something about the way Gordon Cleave was lurking in the shadow of that Channel Four van that sent a chill through me.

There's something else, too, something that could just as easily have been a trick of the sunlight, but I would bet my life I saw Gordon fiddling with something in his pocket, something about the size of my palm. I could have sworn it glowed.

Then, like a voice from on high, the speakers at the entrance boom.

"Ladies and gentlemen, welcome to the grand opening of the GOLDEN APPLE AMUSEMENT PARK!"

The swollen crowd at the entrance roars with cheers, yet somehow even amid the cacophony and unrestrained excitement, I hear my dad say to no one in particular:

"It's started."

I want to see his face, to hear him explain. I want his reassurance. Anything.

But the doors to the park open, and before I know it, I'm swept up in a wave of every family, every couple, every kid, every person in the town of Raven Brooks flocked for the free-admission inaugural day of the park my dad built.

I feel lost in the undertow at first, swirling in place in search of my sister or my parents. I'm overtaken by the lights and music and smells of every ride, prize stand, photo booth, dancing Golden Apple character, screaming child, and sparkling light. There are rides packed into every corner of the place that feels like it was a knot of trees mere days ago. Lines wind and curl around tilt-a-whirls and spinning apple rides and bumper cars. There's Cider Hill, a lower but faster coaster for the brave but little kids; there's the Granny Smith Grotto, the largest confection stand offering every Golden Apple ever made, even the infamous peppermint flavor, which has since become a cult favorite, strangely. There's the Johnny AppleSled, the Fuji Flipper, the Honeycrisp Haunted Hotel, and the *Pink Lady Review* in the enormous amphitheater.

And there at the back of the park—free of the tarp to shield its enormity—stands the Rotten Core in all its horrible glory.

Channel Four is filming its segment, seemingly unaware that they've been scooped by a couple of kids, and finally,

I locate my dad, who is being dragged by Mayor Tavish before the camera for a chat about the coaster.

"Tell the people how you came up with it, Ted," says Mayor Tavish, his arm draped across my dad's shoulders. Mr. Tavish is standing on another box.

"Well, Marvin," my dad says. "I took my last design for a roller coaster and made it bigger."

Mayor Tavish sighs and slices his hand across his throat. "Cut. Don't use that."

"That's not really your call to make, Marv," Chet-cantstopbeingannoying Biggs says, then looks to the news director. "Gordon, what'd you think?"

But the news director isn't paying attention. He's distracted, staring off in the direction of the forest I recognize immediately as the same place where we found the nest. My eyes fall to his pocket, where Gordon Cleave is still holding tight to something.

He isn't just distracted, though. He looks almost nervous.

Mayor Tavish seems to notice this, too, and tries coolly leading the news director to the edge of the park, away from prying ears.

My dad sees it, though, and now he and I are both pretending we can read lips. Gordon Cleave doesn't just look nervous, though. He looks downright frightened.

Which was how my dad looked only a few minutes ago, but now he looks as confused as I feel, and why does this all just seem to be getting more complicated?

"There you are!" Mya says, screeching to a halt beside me. She's panting from her sprint, flanked by Maritza and Lucy on either side of her. "C'mon! We're gonna ride the monster, and so are you."

I squint into the sun and search for the apex of the Rotten Core.

"Not a chance."

"Come *on*, Aaron!" Mya pleads.

"Thanks, but I like my stomach in my, uh, stomach."

Mya rolls her eyes.

"Is it okay, Dad?"

Dad isn't listening, though. He's too busy failing to lip-read.

"Dad?"

"Hmm?"

"The Rotten Core! Can we?"

Dad doesn't turn around. He doesn't dare break focus.

"Yeah, yeah. Sure, hon. Sure."

Mya barely hears the approval before she's off.

Mayor Tavish breaks away from Gordon before the news director has finished what he was saying, which seems to enrage Gordon Cleave, but Mayor Tavish only has eyes for Dad in this moment.

"Let's try one more time, Teddy."

"Ted."

Mayor Tavish forces a smile. "This time, maybe . . . a little more enthusiasm. Some of that trademark creativity, eh?"

Dad grits his teeth and reluctantly follows the mayor back to his box, eventually tearing his eyes from Gordon Cleave.

But I don't.

The second the cameras begin to roll and he thinks no one is looking, Gordon backs into the thicket of trees at the park's perimeter.

"I told you he wouldn't be on the coaster," Enzo says as he and Trinity approach from behind. "He's got a brain in his head."

"Thanks," I say, distracted. Where did Cleave go?

"We're trying the Ferris wheel. Slow and caged-in. My kinda ride," Enzo says. "You coming?"

"Hmmm?"

"Whoa, all you need is an argyle sweater and a 'stache, and you're a scrawny version of your dad."

I blink back into focus.

"What?" I say, turning like I've never laid eyes on Enzo or Trinity before.

Enzo shakes his head. "Okay. We're going to leave you to stare into space now. Weirdo."

Trinity smiles. "We'll come find you after the wheel."

I'm not thinking about wheels or argyle sweaters, though. I'm thinking about where Gordon Cleave went in such a hurry, and why he looked so scared.

That's when I see a flash of movement between the

trees at the other edge of the park, close to where we found the nest.

Close to the factory.

I sprint across the asphalt and take a quick glance around to make sure no one sees me, then leap into the forest and keep low to the ground, staying still while I wait for movement. Sure enough, there's Gordon Cleave, dashing from tree to tree like he's late for a very important date, and boy am I on the other side of the looking glass now because the sound of the Golden Apple Amusement Park is growing softer with every stride, and if I'm right, I know exactly where Gordon Cleave is headed.

Skidding to a stop when Cleave stops to take a breather, I dip my head between my knees behind a tree to catch my own breath. When I pop my head back up, the director is nowhere to be seen.

"Dang it!"

I creep up to the place he'd been standing, and even though I don't see him, I can see clearly where he's tromped through the overgrowth. There's no question now—he's headed to the factory.

Which means he's headed to the tunnels.

The basement door to the factory should be shut. It *would* be shut if not for the clump of grass and dirt acting as a doorstop.

I ease it open slowly and wait for my eyes to adjust to the

dark before pulling in one sweet breath, then tiptoe toward the stairwell leading to the tunnels.

From here, I'll have to move more carefully. In these tunnels, you can hear everything.

I don't have to try too hard to mask my footsteps, though, because Gordon Cleave is running at full speed, careless about his own noise, which at least tells me he doesn't know I'm following him.

Yet.

We reach a familiar bend in the tunnels, then another, and before I know it, we're back to the weather station, but not through the first passage I discovered. This one is the path we found that night, when we discovered the first one was boarded up.

Gordon Cleave seems to know these tunnels like he's traveled them before.

The knot in my stomach travels to my throat, and I stop to find my breath, aware that Gordon Cleave's steps are getting farther and farther away.

"What are you doing?" I scold myself.

Then I remember the look on my dad's face this morning in the kitchen. I remember the way he reached across the table for my mom's hand, the way his voice sounded.

He was the dad he used to be.

And then I know what I'm doing here, why I'm standing in a dank tunnel following a man I don't know to a place I can only guess.

I'm getting my dad back.

I'm in the weather station before I can fully catch my breath again, and I realize that I don't hear footsteps anymore. I do, however, see a dim light coming from my grandparents' office.

Resisting the urge to barge in and tell him to unhand my grandparents' things, I wait in the shadows of the hallway until the news director extinguishes his light and reemerges. I press my back against the wall and watch him crouch, then pull with all his might against the boards blocking the tunnel entrance.

After he does finally pry them away, he drops through the opening, and when I think enough time has passed to avoid detection, I follow him.

Straight to the observatory.

The weather station was one thing. I somehow feel more at home there. Maybe it's because at one point, my grandparents felt at home there.

The observatory is another story. This isn't my place. This belongs to someone else.

I peer into the opening and try to see what Gordon Cleave was in such a hurry to get here for, but with the floors not doing their weird glowing thing, I can't see.

What about the windows?

I look up toward what was a glass ceiling the other night, but impossibly, the entire window is now solid stone.

"What?"

The word escapes my lips before I can stop it.

Gordon Cleave's head snaps toward the passage opening, and I try to duck, but my knee hits rock, and something shifts. A chunk of the lip curving around the bottom of the passage shakes loose, and for the second time in so many days, I'm falling through the opening to the observatory, landing hard on the ground.

Then I'm staring at Gordon Cleave, his hulking shadow even more threatening than it had been in the corner of my basement.

He's holding the abandoned black cloak, raven's feathers poking up from the lining like spines.

This is the exact moment when I realize I have no plan. I knew why I was here, sure. But not what I would do.

Now I'm trapped in an underground room with a potentially dangerous man. And no one knows where I am.

As though reading my thoughts, Gordon Cleave lets a wide grin spread slowly across his face. It's the first time I've ever seen a smile on this man's face. There are some people who were not made to smile, and he's one of them.

"Kid, you have no idea what you've stumbled into," he says, a deep, crackling laugh seeping from his mouth.

My knees feel like they might give out, and I struggle to stand straight. I struggle to breathe. My smart mouth, though, never seems to struggle.

"Enlighten me."

He laughs again, which fails to send the same icy chill through me as it did the first time.

Maybe it's dumb, or naive, or whatever, but I feel excited. Finally, *finally*, I'm going to get some answers.

"You should be so lucky, little man. Or rather, *I* should be so lucky."

I wait, knowing he's trying to bait me. If I let him talk just a little more, maybe he'll say something important.

It isn't anything he says that sheds light on the truth, though. It's the glowing from his pocket—the glowing that forms the same pattern as the green and purple lights on the floor of the observatory.

The room begins to rumble the way it did the other night.

"You ever wondered, Peterson boy, if your family is cursed?" Gordon Cleave grins.

The floor shakes and sways, and the grooves glow, and the device Gordon Cleave now holds in his hand burns bright, and, all at once, I am not here.

I'm at *Fernweh Welt*, sprinting up the slick ramp of the doomed flume ride.

I'm in the forest, peering over the shoulders of my friends and sister as we read the words scrawled all over the rides of the Golden Apple Amusement Park.

I'm staring up at the tallest roller coaster I've ever seen, staring at the word "CURSED," paint dripping like blood down the rails and beams, a fatal omen of my dad's creation.

I'm standing in the park on opening day, the sun shining down bright as I watch Maritza, Lucy, and my sister take their place at the front of the line.

"MYA!"

The device in Gordon Cleave's hand suddenly flashes a hot white that steals my sight. I hear the hard clink of brass on rock and recover in time to see Cleave crouching by his cloak, clutching at his eyes.

But I don't care about the device. And I don't care about Gordon Cleave.

I take a running leap toward the chunk of stone that fell to the floor and grasp the now lower bottom of the passage's opening, vaulting myself back into the tunnel and sprinting through the dark. I retrace every surreptitious step through the passages chanting a single name.

"Mya. Mya."

As though that might save her. As though I might keep her from climbing into that very first car.

"Mya!"

I crash through the opening to the weather station and through the tunnel leading to the factory. I throw the basement door open and couldn't care less who sees me. I bound through the forest and let the blackberry vines shred my legs. I will not stop until I reach the park, even if it means my lungs implode.

Then, time suddenly slows to an agonizing stop. A single

raven from high in a tree above screeches its cry, sending a million smaller crows scattering from the neighboring trees like sparks from a firecracker.

The air is heavy and quiet.

And then there's a single, small, quick, horrifying, ear-splitting scream . . .

About the Author

Photo credit: Kristyn Stroble

CARLY ANNE WEST is the author of the YA novels *The Murmurings* and *The Bargaining*. She holds an MFA in English and Writing from Mills College and lives with her husband and two kids near Portland, Oregon. Visit her at www.carlyannewest.com.